AF408010

Murder at the Bee Farm

Sue Hollowell

Murder at the Bee Farm

Copyright © 2024 Sue Hollowell. All rights reserved.

This is a work of fiction. Names, characters, places, and incidents either are the product of the author's imagination or are used fictitiously. Any resemblance to actual persons, living or dead, events or locales is entirely coincidental. All rights reserved.

This book or any portion thereof may not be reproduced or used in any manner whatsoever without the express written permission of the publisher.

Cover by Lou Harper at coveraffairs.com

Contents

Chapter One

The tires of my beat-up sedan crunched over the gravel driveway as I pulled up to the Sunny Honey B&B, its stately Victorian facade bathed in the golden light of late afternoon. I sat there for a moment, staring up at the peaked gables and ornate trim work that adorned the old house. It looked just as I remembered it, a vision plucked straight from the pages of a fairytale book.

With a deep breath, I stepped out of the car. The early autumn air was crisp but carried a lingering scent of honey and wildflowers. I grabbed my duffle bag from the back seat and made my way up the front steps. My heart pounded as I raised my hand to ring the bell. I hadn't seen my grandmother Iris in over a year, not since that disastrous Thanksgiving when I first brought Chase home to meet her.

The heavy oak door swung open and there stood Grandma, as elegant and vibrant as ever. Her steel gray hair was swept up in its signature bun and her eyes, the same deep green as mine, crinkled at the corners as she broke into a wide smile.

"Moxie, my dear girl!" she cried, pulling me into a warm embrace. "It's so good to see you."

I melted into her familiar floral scent mixed with traces of cinnamon and nutmeg. It was the smell of home.

"Hi Grandma," I said, my voice muffled against her shoulder.

She held me at arm's length; her gaze searching my face. I attempted a brave smile, but her expression immediately softened with understanding.

"Oh sweetie, come inside. Let's get you settled." She grabbed my hand and led me through the door.

I followed her into the cozy front parlor, my eyes roaming over the familiar furnishings. Plush antique chairs were arranged in conversational clusters, while the fireplace mantel held an assortment of framed photos chronicling generations of family memories. Vases of fresh wildflowers and potted herbs added cheerful pops of color.

"Welcome back," she said, giving my arm an affectionate squeeze. "I've kept your old room just as you left it."

My heart swelled with gratitude. After everything that had happened, it felt good to be somewhere familiar, where I knew I was loved.

"Thanks Grandma. I really appreciate you taking me in like this."

"Nonsense, you're always welcome here." She cocked her head, regarding me fondly. "Now, why don't I fix us some tea while you get settled?"

I nodded and headed upstairs to my childhood bedroom on the third floor overlooking the back garden. Pushing open the white washed door, I was flooded with nostalgia. The walls were still a cheerful robin's egg blue and my white iron bed was neatly made with the eyelet lace bedspread Grandma had sewn for my tenth birthday.

I sank down on the edge of the bed and glanced around. Well-worn paperbacks filled the bookshelves, ranging from Nancy Drew mysteries to classics like Pride and Prejudice. My old beloved teddy bear, Patch, sat in the window seat next to a vase of fresh daisies. It was like stepping back in time.

After leaving the duffle bag on the bed, I went over to the window and peered out. The garden looked just as magical as I remembered, blooming with late summer blossoms. I could see the stone path winding its way between flower beds and arching trellises, leading to the pond and gazebo tucked against the back hedge.

As I was taking in the view, a flash of movement caught my eye. I looked down to see a large gray tabby prowling along the garden wall, long tail swishing languidly. He stretched, then sat back on his haunches and glanced up at the window. Our eyes met, and the cat's intense golden gaze struck me.

"Well hello there," I murmured. "Aren't you handsome?"

The cat blinked slowly, as if in response. I smiled. Maybe this cozy B&B with its charming garden was just the fresh start I needed.

Venturing back downstairs, I found Grandma in the sunroom, laying out an assortment of scones, biscotti, and finger sandwiches. A teapot steeped on a vintage side table set for two.

"There you are, dear," she said, setting down a tray of tea cakes. "Come sit and tell me all about what you've been up to this past year."

I settled into an armchair upholstered in rose-patterned fabric. Grandma took the seat opposite and began preparing our cups.

"Oh, you know, the usual," I replied vaguely, not quite ready to delve into the actual reasons behind my sudden return. Chase's betrayal was still too raw. Just thinking about it made my stomach knot with anger and hurt.

Sensing my reluctance, she smoothly changed the subject. "The hydrangeas are especially lovely this year, and the kitchen herb garden has been flourishing. Oh, remember your old high school friend? Samantha? She's now the town reporter for the Nectar News."

"Oh?" I replied. Samantha, "Sammy" and I didn't end our relationship well when I escaped the small town for the big city. She thought I had gone out with her boyfriend. Turns out her boyfriend was sweet on me, but I never returned the feelings. Sammy believed him over me and resented me.

I nodded politely as Grandma caught me up on happenings around the B&B, welcoming the distraction. We chatted about renovations to the third floor suites, the upcoming schedule of cooking classes, and the seasonal menu updates.

As we finished our tea and snacks, I noticed the cat from the garden prowling near the sunroom's open French doors. Iris followed my gaze.

"Don't mind Sneaker," she said. "He's a stray who turned up a few months back. I don't want a pet, so don't feed him. He'll never leave if you do."

"Sneaker?" I asked with a laugh.

Grandma smiled. "Because he sneaks up so quietly. Nearly gave Betty a heart attack when she found him on the kitchen counter one morning!"

I chuckled at the thought of startling one of the B&B's elderly residents. Betty and her husband George were fixtures around here, having lived at the Sunny Honey B&B for nearly a decade.

Right on cue, I heard bickering voices and turned to see Betty and George shuffling into the sunroom. Betty's powder blue sweater set and George's red cardigan made them look like walking Valentine's candy.

"Oh wonderful, you have tea prepared!" Betty said. "George and I could use a nice hot cup."

The couple settled onto the loveseat, Betty smoothing her floral print skirt while George adjusted his glasses and crossed his ankles. I hid a smile. Some things never changed.

"Moxie, dear! When did you get here?" Betty asked, finally noticing me.

"Just this afternoon. It's nice to see you both again," I said.

"Well, we're just delighted you've come back," said George, his eyes twinkling benevolently behind thick spectacles. "Your grandmother kept your room exactly the same. We told her you'd be back one day!"

Grandma smiled affectionately as she poured tea for her long-time guests. "Yes, yes, you two are always right. Now drink up before it gets cold."

We had a pleasant hour of eating and chatting. Betty and George regaled us with funny stories about their toy poodle's latest antics and reminisced about memorable guests from over the years. I relaxed, caught up in their familiar rapport.

As afternoon faded to evening, I helped Grandma clear the tea service, then retreated upstairs to continue unpacking. I hung clothes in the carved oak armoire and lined up my favorite books on the shelves. Slipping on comfy pajamas, I peered out the window once more. Dusk was falling, casting dusky purple shadows across the garden. Somewhere out there Sneaker was likely prowling the night, another stray finding solace here. The thought was oddly comforting.

I was just crawling into bed with a book when there was a soft knock and Grandma entered, bearing a glass of warm milk.

"Thank you," I said, taking it from her outstretched hands.

She perched on the edge of the bed and brushed a strand of hair from my face. "Feeling any better, my dear?"

I stared down into the pale milk, blinking back sudden tears. She didn't push, just waited patiently for me to gather my thoughts.

Finally I whispered, "Chase cheated on me. That's why I left." Saying the words out loud somehow made them real.

Grandma inhaled sharply. "That fool. I never did trust him."

A chuckle escaped me. "I know. I should have listened to you."

She squeezed my hand, her lined face creased in sympathy. "We all make mistakes in love. What matters is picking ourselves up again. You're young and strong, Moxie. This too shall pass."

I managed a small smile. "Thanks, Grandma. You always know just what to say."

We sat in cozy silence for a few minutes. She gave my hand one final pat and stood.

"Get some rest now. You've got a big day tomorrow with the training."

After she left, I snuggled under the covers with my book, too distracted to focus on the words. My mind kept replaying those last awful moments with Chase - the confusion, the tears, the shattered illusion of our future. With a heavy sigh, I set the book aside and switched off the light. Maybe starting over at the Sunny Honey B&B was exactly what I needed to mend my broken heart.

***

I woke to buttery sunlight streaming through the lace curtains. Downstairs, I could hear the muted sounds of guests chatting and silverware clinking over breakfast in the dining room. Stretching luxuriously, I took my time getting ready, enjoying having nowhere in particular to rush off to.

After a long shower, I headed out to the garden, breathing deeply of the late summer air. Early sunlight dappled the gravel paths, and birds chirped merrily in the leafy branches overhead. I wandered over to inspect the herbs, running my fingers over fuzzy sage, feathery dill fronds, and pungent thyme. Tugging a few mint leaves, I popped them in my mouth, savoring the burst of fresh flavor.

Continuing deeper into the garden, I paused by the fishpond, trailing my fingers through the cool water. Koi in gleaming shades of coral, gold, and white drifted lazily beneath the surface. As I skirted a bank of purple asters, a flash of movement again caught my eye. I turned to see the gray tabby step gracefully from the shadows. He trotted right over and began twining figure eights around my ankles, rumbling happily.

"Well hello Sneaker," I chuckled, bending down to scratch behind his ears. "Did you sleep well out here?"

The cat arched into my hand, slitted eyes drifting closed in contentment. Emboldened, he gave my fingers an affectionate lick.

"Alright you, let's get some breakfast too." I stood, brushing cat hair from my jeans, and headed back inside, Sneaker padding silently behind me.

Once I confirmed that Grandma and the guests were engaged in the dining room, I quietly moved towards the kitchen. My heart raced. I had told myself not to get attached to Sneaker, the stray cat, but it was hard not to.

The kitchen door creaked as I opened it. Inside, it was warm and smelled of breakfast leftovers. I checked for any signs of movement, hearing only the refrigerator humming.

I grabbed a stool to reach the top shelf where Grandma kept the tuna. She was strict about not feeding Sneaker, worried he'd never leave if we did. I quietly took down the tin and headed back to the door, trying to be as silent as possible.

A soft meow came from the window. Sneaker was there, looking right at me. I opened the tin and put some tuna on a saucer. Opening the back door just a crack, I set the saucer on the stoop. Sneaker came right over and started eating.

"Don't expect this every time," I whispered, smiling despite myself. I felt a connection to the stray, both of us needing a bit of kindness.

I quickly washed the saucer and returned it, making sure everything looked untouched. As I closed the door, Sneaker's purrs were soft but happy. Our little secret was safe.

I headed to the dining room, where breakfast was still in full swing. I grabbed some scrambled eggs and sourdough bread and joined a table near the window.

"Have you heard about the honey-tasting contest they're adding this year?" Betty asked, her voice filled with enthusiasm.

George nodded, his interest piqued. "I'm actually more excited to see the live beekeeping demo. It's amazing how they manage the hives and collect the honey."

The upcoming honey festival at Sweet Buzz Farms seemed to be the talk of the day.

After the breakfast crowd had thinned and the last of the guests wandered off to start their day, Grandma and I cleared the tables.

"We'll start with the reservation book," she said as we loaded the dishwasher. "It's practically an antique, so it fits right in here." She winked, leading me to the aged leather-bound book on the front desk.

I watched, amused, as she flipped through pages filled with elegant cursive. "This," she declared, "is what I call high-tech. None of that newfangled digital mess can replace the charm of handwritten notes!"

I bit my lip, trying not to giggle as she donned a pair of oversized reading glasses. "First rule of night clerking: if you can't find it in here, it probably doesn't exist."

"Got it," I replied, my voice laced with a laugh. "Trust the book."

"Exactly!" She patted the ledger fondly. "Now, let's pretend to check in a guest." Grandma picked up an old rotary phone and pretended it was ringing. "Sunny Honey B&B, how may I help you?" she chirped into the receiver. She paused, nodding sagely to an imaginary caller. "Ah, Mr. and Mrs. Smith! We have your usual room ready. The one without those pesky modern comforts like Wi-Fi."

I covered my mouth with my hand, stifling a laugh. Grandma placed the receiver down and shot me a mischievous grin. "People come here for the rustic charm, Moxie. Who needs Wi-Fi when you have the great outdoors and good company?"

Next, she moved on to show me the 'computer system'--an ancient desktop that hummed and whirred like it was powering up for a space launch. "This old beast is more decoration than utility. But occasionally, it behaves."

I chuckled as she poked at the keyboard with theatrical suspicion, as if it might bite. "Sometimes, I sweet-talk it just right, and it lets me check my emails."

"Does it have a name?" I asked, playing along with her light-hearted training session.

"Gertrude," she replied instantly. "Stubborn, but reliable after she gets going."

By the time we finished our lesson, my cheeks ached from smiling so much, and my heart was full of appreciation for the unique charm Grandma brought to every detail of running the B&B. I was learning more than just the tasks; I was learning the heart of hospitality, Iris style.

CHAPTER TWO

I made my way downstairs, my heart fluttering with a mix of excitement and trepidation. This was it - my first official night shift at the Sunny Honey B&B.

"There you are, dear." Grandma emerged from the parlor, a warm smile lighting up her face. She looked as poised as ever in a floral print dress cinched at the waist with a string of pearls. "Are you ready for your maiden voyage into the world of night clerking?"

I took a deep, steadying breath and nodded. "As ready as I'll ever be, I suppose."

She gave my arm an affectionate pat. "You'll do just fine. Now, let's go over a few key things one more time."

She led me behind the polished oak front desk and pulled out a thick, leather-bound book. "This is where you'll log all your overnight arrivals and departures. Be sure to note any special requests or room assignments."

Flipping it open, I ran my fingers over the delicate pages covered in her elegant cursive. The faint aroma of aged paper and ink wafted up, making me smile. There was something so charmingly tactile about this old-fashioned way of doing things.

Next, she handed me a well-worn ring of keys, each one labeled with a hand-written tag. "These open every guest room, as well as the back entrances and storage areas. Guard them with your life!" She winked conspiratorially. "Seriously though, they're priceless."

I jangled the ring, marveling at the various shapes and sizes - some ornate, others plain but clearly dating back decades. "Got it. No losing the keys."

"Last," Grandma said, producing a battered address book from beneath the counter, "this has all our important contacts. Should anything go wrong - and I mean anything at all - these are the folks to call."

She flipped through the pages, pointing out various names and numbers with a perfectly manicured nail. Plumbers, electricians, locksmiths - even a 24-hour glass repair service, just in case. Finally, she tapped one name that seemed to be a central fixture: Frankie Miller.

"Frankie is our miracle worker. Handyman extraordinaire, who knows this place better than anyone aside from me. Whatever breaks, whatever goes bump in the night, he's the one to ring first."

I committed the name and number to memory, already feeling reassured by the idea of having a local expert on call.

"I'll leave you to settle in," Grandma said, giving my shoulder an affectionate squeeze. "But I'm just down the hall if you need anything at all. You've got this, Moxie."

As her footsteps faded away, I took a deep breath and glanced around, familiarizing myself with my new domain. The front desk area was small but cozy, with polished hardwood floors and a sitting area furnished with overstuffed armchairs and sofas. A stone fireplace anchored one corner, all that remained lit by the crackling flames and a few well-placed lamps. It had such an inviting, homey ambiance - I could already envision guests lingering here with a book and a glass of wine before retiring for the evening.

Settling into the worn leather desk chair, I flipped open the logbook to the current date, scanning the list of occupied rooms and notations about early arrivals. According to Grandma's tidy script, we were nearly at capacity for the weekend. I double checked that each room had been properly refreshed and stocked, making a few notes of my own about extra towels or amenities some guests had requested.

As the evening stretched on, I fielded a handful of calls - one booking a last-minute romantic getaway, another asking about local hiking trails. Each time the old brass phone rang, I felt a tiny thrill, as if I were truly taking my first steps into the hospitality world. By the time I checked in my first guests - a cheerful young couple celebrating their anniversary - I had begun to relax into the easy rhythm of the job.

The soft trill of the doorbell broke the peaceful quiet around 10 pm. I glanced up to see a stout, middle-aged man stamping his work boots on the mat, knocking off clods of reddish dirt. He had a craggy, sun-weathered face topped with a fraying baseball cap emblazoned with the word 'Miller's' in peeling letters. Based on his rumpled coveralls and well-used tool belt, I had a hunch who this might be.

"Good evening," I greeted as he ambled up to the desk. "Can I help you?"

The man's eyes crinkled at the corners as he broke into a broad grin. "Well hey there, you must be Iris's granddaughter Moxie that I've heard so much about!"

I couldn't help but return his warm smile. "That's me. And you're Frankie Miller, I'm guessing?"

"The one and only!" He chuckled, leaning against the counter. "Your grandma said you'd be flyin' solo tonight for the first time. Just wanted to poke my head in and make sure you're all settled."

"I appreciate that," I replied sincerely. Already, this friendly face helped put me more at ease. "Though I have to admit, I'm wondering what kind of trouble a quaint place like this could get into after hours."

Frankie snorted. "You'd be surprised. This old gal's got a mind of her own." He patted the desktop fondly. "Comes with the territory when you're an antique, I reckon."

"Is that so?" I asked, intrigued. "I'd love to hear some stories sometime."

"Oh, I've got plenty of those," he assured me with a wink. "For now, though, I'm actually here on business. Got a call earlier today about a leaky shower head up on the third floor, room thirty-two. I'm sorry to be here so late."

I quickly referenced the log. "Looks like that's Mr. and Mrs. Caldwell's room. Let me grab the key."

As I fished out the proper key and made a note about the repair, Frankie leaned against the desk, hands stuffed into his pockets.

"You hear any buzz about that ruckus out at Sweet Buzz Farms?" he asked in a low voice.

I paused, keys jangling softly as I looked up. "No, what happened?"

He shook his head slowly. "Ah, you know how folks like to gossip in a small town like this. Probably nothin' but I heard there was some kinda disturbance out there. Cops sniffin' around the bee farm and all."

My curiosity was instantly piqued. Sweet Buzz was one of the local farms that took part in the annual Honey Festival - an event I'd been looking forward to experiencing again.

"A disturbance? Like what, vandalism or something?" I asked.

Frankie spread his hands. "Heck if I know. You'd have to ask that reporter, Sammy what's-her-name. She's always sniffin' around for a scoop."

I made a mental note to track down Sammy once I had a free moment. Any potential drama surrounding the festival was sure to make for an interesting news story - and a lively bit of town gossip, too.

"Anywho, I'd best get to work on that shower before those Cald-wells flood the whole third floor." Frankie pushed off from the counter with a grunt. "Don't be a stranger now, you hear?"

With a parting wink and the jingle of his tool belt, the genial handy-man headed off down the hall. I watched him go.

The rest of my shift passed relatively uneventfully. A few more guests filtered in to check-in, including one elderly couple who ex-citedly regaled me with their anticipation of the upcoming Honey Festival events.

"We've been coming every year for the last decade," the woman declared in a wavery voice. "My Harold just loves watching the bee-keepers work. Don't you, dear?"

Her husband, stooped and balding beneath a newsboy cap, nodded enthusiastically. "Fascinating stuff, that honey-making business! Did you know that to produce just one pound of honey, the bees have to tap over two million flowers?"

I chuckled at their unbridled eagerness, making a note to pick the old man's brain for more fun bee facts. Maybe I could incorporate some into the storytelling event I was mulling over.

By the time the wee hours rolled around, a hush had settled over the B&B. I passed the time alternating between reviewing the guest logs and stealing occasional glances out the front windows. The grounds were bathed in silvery moonlight, the shadows of the oak trees stretching in slanting patterns across the gardens. It was so tranquil, almost haunting in its utter stillness.

A soft 'mrrp' broke the quiet, and I glanced down to see Sneaker emerge from the shadows, yellow eyes gleaming. He blinked up at me lazily before sauntering over to wind his way around my ankles.

"Hey there," I murmured, bending to give him an affectionate scratch behind the ears. "How did you get inside?"

The tabby rumbled contentedly, arching into my touch with undisguised delight. I couldn't help but smile - it was like the curmudgeonly old cat had decided to keep me company during these long, lonely hours.

Sneaking him a few treats from the small stash I'd squirreled away, I settled onto the sofa in front of the fireplace, Sneaker hopping up to curl beside me. His deep, rumbling purrs filled the stillness as I slowly turned the pages of the guest book, reading over the brief notations and comments left by previous clerks.

One entry in particular caught my eye - a handwritten addendum beside the room number for one of our most frequent guests, Mr. Leonard Griffith.

"Enjoys discussing ancient timepieces and all things mechanical. Be sure to engage on this. A true expert!"

I raised an eyebrow, intrigued. Clearly, this was a quirky individual with some fascinating knowledge to share. I'd have to make a point of introducing myself properly.

As the night inched towards morning, I began prepping for the breakfast rush, ensuring the dining room was tidy and the coffee carafes freshly brewed. The scent of rich Arabica soon filled the air, mingling with the wood smoke from the fireplace in an utterly inviting way.

I was just setting out the bakery basket filled with fresh croissants and muffins when I heard the soft tread of footsteps in the hall. A moment later, Grandma swept in, somehow looking as fresh and put-together as she had the previous afternoon.

"Good morning, dear," she greeted warmly. "How was your first solo flight?"

I couldn't contain my grin as I recounted the night's events - the minor plumbing repair, the enthusiastic Honey Festival fans. She shook her head in mild disapproval.

"That cat is nothing but trouble, I swear. If you're not careful, he'll worm his way right into your heart," she said.

Her eyes danced with amusement, letting me know she wasn't truly upset. If anything, she seemed pleased to see me fitting in so naturally. I knew then this was exactly where I needed to be while putting my life back together.

As the breakfast crowd trickled in, I took a moment to review the service log, making notes of any special requests or areas that might need extra attention from the housekeeping staff. I was just contemplating how best to pitch my idea for a storytelling event when a new voice rang out.

"Well, well, if it isn't Moxie Rayburn!" a familiar voice called out with a hint of sarcasm. "I was wondering when you'd come slinking back into town."

I glanced up to see Sammy Williams leaning against the desk, her trademark fiery curls pulled back into a messy bun. She was impeccably dressed, as always, in a smart blazer and slacks, undoubtedly ready to chase down her next big scoop for the Nectar News.

My smile faltered slightly at her biting tone. Sammy and I went way back, but things had been tense between us ever since the disastrous fallout over that rumor about me and her high school boyfriend. I had tried to explain the truth, but she never believed me over him.

"Nice to see you too, Sammy," I replied evenly, refusing to rise to the bait. "I didn't realize you were covering the hospitality beat these days."

She rolled her eyes exaggeratedly. "Please, you know I'll report on anything that bleeds - or in this case, leads." Her eyes narrowed as she looked me over appraisingly. "Though I have to admit, I'm surprised the mighty Moxie lowered herself to come back to this podunk little town."

The jab stung, but I refused to let it show. "What can I say? I missed Grandma's home cooking," I quipped lightly.

Sammy scoffed. "Sure you did. Speaking of which, I heard through the grapevine that Iris lured me here to interview one of the guests? Some old coot who's an 'expert' on ancient clocks or something?"

I bristled at her dismissive tone regarding Leonard. "For your information, Mr. Griffith is an incredibly knowledgeable horologist. But I wouldn't expect someone like you to appreciate that."

Sammy's eyes flashed dangerously. We both knew I was referring to her tendency to prioritize flashy stories over substance. An awkward silence stretched between us, laden with unresolved tensions.

Finally, she tapped her pen against her notebook with a tight smile. "Well, aren't you just a wealth of useful information now that you're playing innkeeper? Maybe you're not as useless as I thought."

With that parting barb, she pushed off from the counter and strutted away, every bit the confrontational reporter on the hunt for her next big break. I watched her go, my hands clenched into fists at my sides.

No matter how much time passed, Sammy always knew exactly which buttons to push. Worse, part of me worried she might be right - maybe I didn't have what it took to make a real go of things here after all. Shoving aside those insecure thoughts, I took a deep, steadying breath.

I was through letting Sammy Williams get under my skin. This was my fresh start, and I was determined not to let anything, or anyone, derail me.

The rest of the breakfast rush passed in a blur of coffee refills, clearing plates, and exchanging friendly banter with the guests. I was just settling in for a rare lull when a distinguished-looking gentleman approached the desk.

Despite the morning hour, he wore an impeccably dressed linen suit, precisely combed silver hair, and neatly trimmed beard. Peering at me over half-moon spectacles, his gaze was both warm and inquisitive.

"You must be the new night clerk I've been hearing so much about," he said in a rich, cultured tone. "Leonard Griffith, at your service."

He extended his hand, and I shook it, oddly charmed by his old-world courtesy.

"Moxie Rayburn. It's a pleasure to meet you, Mr. Griffith," I said. "I've heard a lot about you."

"Please, Leonard," he insisted with a gentle smile. "I'm an old friend of the Sunny Honey B&B and have no need for such formalities."

His gaze drifted to the row of vintage timepieces Grandma had displayed on the high shelves behind the desk - an assortment of ornate mantle clocks, gilded and carved into fanciful shapes. I watched the realization dawn across his face.

"Ah, I see you've discovered my little hobby!" he said.

I glanced up at the clocks, instantly intrigued. "Are those all antiques? They're stunning."

Leonard's face positively glowed with enthusiasm. "Indeed, they are! I'm a horologist by trade - a studier and repairer of timepieces, if you will. Iris lets me display those particular specimens as just a small sample from my personal collection."

"You collect antique clocks?" I asked, both impressed and fascinated. "That's incredible. They must be chock full of history."

"My dear, you have no idea," he agreed with undisguised zeal. "Why, that carriage clock there on the end, that's an exquisite example of early 20th century French enameling. See the intricate floral detailing? Utterly sublime. And just wait until you hear the story behind how I acquired it!"

By the time Leonard concluded his reminiscence, I knew I had to incorporate him into my planned storytelling event somehow. His unique expertise could make for such a fascinating addition.

"Leonard, I wonder if I might impose upon you for a tremendous favor," I said, feeling uncharacteristically emboldened. "I'm actually in the process of organizing a storytelling evening here at the B&B - a chance for guests and locals to share tales, legends, you know, that sort of thing. Your accounts about acquiring and restoring these incredible timepieces would be perfect! Would you consider being one of the featured storytellers?"

The dapper horologist's eyes widened with surprise behind his spectacles before crinkling warmly at the corners. "Why, I would be absolutely delighted, my dear! What an ingenious idea! Yes, indeed, I shall endeavor to regale your audience with only the most enthralling of my horological escapades."

I couldn't help but beam, hardly daring to believe my good fortune at securing such a naturally talented storyteller. With Leonard on board, my little event was shaping up to be an unqualified success. "I need to get Iris's approval, but I think she'll be on board with it."

CHAPTER THREE

I was just turning back towards the front desk, mentally cataloging my next tasks, when an imposing figure strode through the entrance. A man in a crisp police uniform cut an authoritative presence, his gaze sweeping the lobby with a scrutinizing intensity that instantly set me on edge.

"Can I help you, officer?" I asked, unable to mask my surprise at his unannounced arrival.

His expression remained inscrutable as he approached the counter, removing his hat in a gesture of polite formality that seemed at odds with the sudden tension crackling between us. "Ms. Rayburn, I presume? Detective Brandon Wilson."

He extended his hand, which I shook reflexively, my brow furrowing slightly at the unexpected formality. "I'm afraid I have some rather... delicate matters to discuss with you."

A knot of apprehension formed in the pit of my stomach at his grave tone.

Before I could respond, the rhythmic tap of Grandma's cane preceded her entrance, her brow furrowed with concern as she took in the detective's presence.

"Brandon," she said, her usual warmth shadowed by a guarded curiosity. "Is everything all right?"

He inhaled deeply, as if steeling himself. "I'm not sure there's an easy way to say this, but I'm afraid I have some disturbing news." His gaze locked with mine, holding me in place with its intensity. "There's been a murder."

The words seemed to suck all the air from the room as dread coiled inside me like a venomous serpent. A murder. Here, in this idyllic little town?

"What happened?" I heard myself ask, my voice barely above a whisper.

Brandon's expression remained impassive, but I detected a glimmer of something like regret in his eyes. "The victim was a young woman named Elena Martinez. She was found late last night out at Sweet Buzz Farms during the festival setup."

Elena. The name triggered a faint spark of recognition, but I couldn't quite place the connection. Grandma, however, visibly recoiled as if struck.

"Elena... the Martinez family has been suppliers for the Honey Festival for decades," she murmured, her face ashen. "Such a sweet girl. Who could possibly..."

She trailed off, seemingly too horror-struck to give voice to the question we were both silently asking. Brandon's jaw tightened grimly.

"That's just it, ma'am. This wasn't any random act." He paused, as if bracing himself. "We have reason to believe Ms. Martinez's murder may have been motivated by... a romantic entanglement."

My breath caught in my throat as realization took insidious root. No. Surely he couldn't mean--

"During the initial sweep of the crime scene, officers recovered the victim's purse," Brandon continued in a measured tone. "Among its contents was a scrap of paper... with your name and phone number written on it, Ms. Rayburn."

The words landed like a physical blow, stealing what little air remained in my lungs. I could only gape at him, my mind utterly blank but for the thunderous pounding of my heart.

"That's... that's impossible," I finally choked out, shaking my head vehemently. "I didn't even know Elena, let alone..."

"Nevertheless, the evidence clearly links you to the victim in some manner," Brandon stated, his voice hardening slightly with professionalism. "Which is why I need to ask... where were you between the hours of ten pm and two am night before last?"

The question, delivered in such a weighted manner, pierced straight through the fog of shock clouding my senses. He was asking for my alibi, treating me as a suspect in this horrific crime.

"I... I was here," I stammered, panic lending a slight tremor to my voice. "You can ask Grandma, she--"

I cut myself off as Brandon's expression remained stubbornly impassive, realizing with a sickening lurch that my grandmother could hardly provide an alibi. She'd been asleep and hadn't seen me after we went to bed.

Grandma seemed to grasp my dilemma as the color drained from her face. "Now see here, Brandon," she interjected, her voice ringing with a protective fierceness that momentarily banished the waver of age. "This is my Moxie you're speaking about. The girl is many things, but a murderer?" She shook her head adamantly. "There must be some mistake."

"I'm not here to make accusations, Iris," Brandon replied, his tone softening somewhat. "But you have to understand, when a victim's personal effects directly implicate someone, we have a responsibility to pursue that lead. Thoroughly."

His gaze bored into me, laden with hesitant apology but unyielding resolve. In that moment, I knew he wasn't simply going through the motions - Brandon genuinely suspected me of being involved in this horrible crime.

The weight of it threatened to crush me utterly.

Grandma opened her mouth, undoubtedly prepared to issue a blistering retort in my defense, but I raised a hand to quiet her. As much as I longed for the sheltering comfort of her trust, I understood the gravity of the situation. If I were to have any hope of clearing my name, I needed to face this head-on.

"You're right, Detective," I said, struggling to keep my voice steady. "I... I wish I could explain how my name and number ended up with the victim, but I honestly have no idea. The truth is, I've been so focused on my new role here at the B&B that I haven't been keeping up with -- with anything else, really."

The unspoken implication hung heavy in the air. Ever since my tumultuous break-up with Chase and the subsequent implosion of my life back in Silver Lake, I'd been operating in a strange sort of cocoon, willfully blind to the world beyond these sheltering walls.

Could it be possible that in my single-minded quest to find solace and redefine myself, I'd somehow crossed paths with Elena Martinez? Try as I might, I could conjure no memory, no plausible scenario that could account for her carrying my information. Unless...

The sickening truth crept upon me like an icy vise around my heart. There was one obvious connection. Could Elena be who Chase cheated on me with?

I had only discovered his infidelity, not the name of the other woman.

Had he, in some fit of twisted vengeance or residual jealousy, given this woman my information? Using me as a pawn in whatever sordid game had culminated in her death? The mere notion made my head spin, dredging up a roiling torrent of emotions I thought I'd successfully buried.

"I need... I need to speak with Chase," I said, as much to myself as to Brandon and Grandma. "Maybe he can shed some light on--"

"Absolutely not!" Grandma's vehement objection sliced through my words with the finality of a guillotine blade. "That miserable snake has caused you enough suffering, Moxie. Getting tangled up with him again would be the gravest mistake you could make!"

I opened my mouth to protest, but she barreled onwards, ire and concern warring across her features.

"Do you honestly think he'd tell you the truth? That he wouldn't simply manipulate you all over again with his lies and excuses?" She shook her head sharply. "No, I won't allow it. We'll find another way to clear your name that doesn't involve reopening old wounds."

Though her words carried the unmistakable sting of truth, I couldn't quash the desperate urge to pursue this potential connection to Chase, no matter how painful. If there was even a chance he could provide the key to absolving me of suspicion in Elena's death, wouldn't I have an obligation to at least try?

"With all due respect, Grandma," I said, fighting to keep my tone measured despite the turmoil churning within me, "if there's any hope of disproving these implications, I have to talk to Chase. No matter how difficult it might be."

Her eyes flashed dangerously, her lips pressed into a rigid line. She opened her mouth, undoubtedly to issue another blistering rebuke, but Brandon cleared his throat, effectively cutting off the confrontation.

"If I may..." He shifted his weight, assuming a diplomatic stance. "I appreciate this is an incredibly difficult situation for you both."

He leveled his gaze at me, his expression inscrutable once more. "I can't officially compel you to make a statement at this stage, but I would strongly advise full cooperation. Whatever insights your... your former partner might provide could potentially go a long way towards clarifying matters."

The words hung heavy between us, a stark reminder of just how precarious my position had become. I was no longer an outsider, blissfully oblivious. I was a person of interest, directly tied to a young woman's murder through means I couldn't fathom.

Squaring my shoulders, I met Brandon's steady gaze with as much conviction as I could muster. "I understand, Detective. And you have my word - I'll do whatever I can to sort this out, no matter where it leads."

His expression remained guarded, but he offered a terse nod of acknowledgment before turning on his heel. I watched him go, feeling as though I'd been hollowed out, utterly unmoored from the sense of hope and purpose I'd awakened with just that morning.

The ominous thud of the door closing behind Brandon seemed to shatter the fragile tension blanketing the lobby. Grandma immediately rounded on me, her eyes blazing with an intensity I'd seldom witnessed from my typically unflappable grandmother.

"Have you lost your senses entirely?" she demanded without pre-amble, advancing towards me with a menacing tap of her cane. "Willingly involving yourself with that wretched boy after everything he's done? It's utter madness!"

I flinched at the venom in her tone. "Grandma, please, you have to understand--"

"I understand you're allowing that serpent to slither his way back into your life with his forked tongue!" she shot back, her words laced with a protective fury. "The things he put you through, the anguish he caused... how can you so easily overlook all of that?"

Her question struck a tender nerve, dredging up memories and emotions I'd fought so hard to repress. I closed my eyes against the onslaught, struggling to regain my equilibrium.

When I finally spoke up, my voice carried a weary resignation. "You're right, Grandma. You're absolutely right - Chase wounded me in ways I'm still recovering from, ways that may never fully heal."

I opened my eyes, met her blazing gaze with one of steady resolution. "But that's exactly why I have to do this. I'm not that same lost, shattered person anymore. I've found strength again, rekindled my sense of self-worth. And I won't let anyone, especially Chase, strip that away from me through intimidation or manipulation."

Grandma searched my expression. After a long, weighted pause, some of the rigidity seemed to bleed from her posture as she exhaled a soft sigh.

"You've always been the most tenacious child," she murmured, a hint of reluctant fondness tempering the worry etched across her face.

A faint smile ghosted across my lips at her oblique acceptance of my resolve. Reaching out, I gave her hand a gentle squeeze.

"I'll be careful, Grandma. I promise," I said.

The words hung in the air, laden with a solemn weight I couldn't quite define.

She searched my expression, seeming to find some reassurance in my resolute candor. Finally, she nodded once more, squeezing my hands tightly. "I have to go see about getting the lunch prep started. I just want the best for you, dear."

I watched her go, grateful I had this wonderful place to return to.

I was just turning my thoughts to mapping out a plan for that inevitably complicated encounter when a familiar voice cut through the stillness.

"Well, if it isn't Moxie spending quality time with the town crackpots," Sammy announced with an exaggerated roll of her eyes as she sauntered up to the desk. "I can't believe Iris actually made me come over here to interview that relic for a puff piece."

I bristled at her dismissive tone regarding Leonard. "Well, I wouldn't expect someone like you to appreciate him," I said.

She scoffed loudly. "Oh, please spare me the lecture on whatever random old man hobby that geezer is into. Talking to him was an absolute waste of my time." She fixed me with a pointed stare. "But then I guess you would know all about wasting time, seeing as you're playing innkeeper instead of accomplishing anything real with your life."

The barb stung, as Sammy's words so often did. Before I could plan a retort, however, she was already turning on her heel with a disdainful sniff.

"Whatever, I've got actual work to do. You just...keep on keeping on with your little innkeeper fantasy." With a toss of her fiery curls, she flounced away, leaving me to seethe in her wake.

I watched her storm off, Sammy's hurtful words still ringing in my ears and reviving old insecurities.

Chapter Four

I waited with my phone in hand, questioning if I was really doing the right thing. Could this decision backfire on me?

My phone pinged, signaling there was no turning back now. A knot of apprehension twisted in my stomach as I saw Chase's name on the screen. "I'll be there in 30," his simple message read, but those words weighed heavily, making it hard to breathe.

I exhaled shakily, steeling my resolve. This was the first concrete step towards uncovering the truth about Elena's death and my alleged involvement. The thought of facing Chase again after our explosive break-up made my heart race.

I tried to convince myself this was merely an investigation now, not an emotional reunion with my ex. That's all this needed to be.

My feet carried me upstairs to my room automatically. I surveyed the contents of my modest closet, mentally debating potential outfits. For a fleeting moment, my eyes landed on the crimson cocktail dress hanging towards the back. The form-fitting silhouette and sweetheart neckline would certainly catch Chase's eye. Coupled with the strappy black heels, I would project a sophisticated allure.

But just as quickly as the thought arose, I dismissed it with an inward scoff. Dressing up for Chase's benefit was the last thing I should be concerned about right now.

Pulling on the soft, broken-in denim, I smiled faintly, remembering when these jeans symbolized my newfound freedom and self-acceptance since my arrival at the B&B. With a fitted sky-blue top, I projected relaxed confidence - someone comfortable in their own skin, unafraid to face challenges head-on.

Yes, I decided with a look in the mirror, a few strokes of mascara and some shimmery lip gloss completing the look. This was the Moxie I wanted Chase to see - reclaimed and grounded in myself, unbowed by his charms or mind games.

As I drove the winding road to the Java Jive cafe to meet Chase, memories of him surfaced that I'd repressed. The accusatory texts and frantic unanswered calls from that fateful night replayed vividly, as did the soul-crushing moment I arrived at his apartment. I could hear a woman's voice and he refused to let me in.

His betrayal had shattered my heart and illusions about our relationship in an instant. The man I loved became a deceitful stranger, capable of calculated lies and heartless disregard for my feelings. I shuddered, gripping the steering wheel tighter to anchor myself in the present.

That was the past, a closed chapter I'd struggled to move on from. And now I was walking back into that minefield, all to uncover the truth about Elena's murder. Was I ready to confront those demons, to look Chase in the eye while dredging up the circumstances that tore us apart?

The Java Jive sign signaled my arrival. With a steadying breath, I parked next to Chase's sleek black coupe. He was already here.

A tremor of trepidation rippled through me as I killed the engine, but I tamped it down. I was Moxie Rayburn, and I would not be intimidated - not by Chase, not by any of this.

I entered the cafe with purpose, the bell tinkling my arrival. Chase sat in the back, looking much the same, yet distinctly different than I remembered. The familiar artfully tousled hair framed weathered features holding a guarded vulnerability that tugged at my hardened heart.

His gaze found mine in a jolt of electric recognition that momentarily stole my breath. A torrent of unspoken words and conflicting emotions flickered across his soulful eyes. Then the moment shattered as he rose, slipping a mask of nonchalance into place.

"Moxie," he greeted, his low rumble sparking an unwanted flutter in my chest. "I'll admit, I didn't expect to hear from you again after..." He cleared his throat. "Well, you know."

I lifted my chin, regarding him through narrowed eyes as I struggled for equilibrium. "Yes, well, circumstances have taken a rather dark turn, wouldn't you agree?"

A flicker of something indecipherable crossed his features before the casual mask resurfaced. "I heard about Elena. Honestly, I'm as shocked as anyone. She didn't seem like the type to make enemies."

There it was - that same practiced nonchalance that had so often disarmed me before. As if he could downplay the situation and divert from the darker implications.

"Really?" I arched a pointed brow, taking the seat opposite him. "Because from where I'm standing, it seems like she made a pretty formidable enemy out of you."

The accusatory words hung heavy between us. Chase's jaw tightened fractionally, the first crack in his facade.

"I don't know what you're implying, Mox, but I can assure you--" he said.

"Don't," I cut him off sharply, making him blink. "Don't insult my intelligence by playing dumb or innocent. We're way past that point."

"Where were you the night Elena was killed?" I asked bluntly, pinning him with a piercing stare.

Chase blinked, caught off guard. "Uh, well, I was...I was at home. Alone. Just a quiet night in, you know how it is."

I arched an incredulous brow. "Alone? You expect me to believe that?"

"It's the truth!" he insisted, a bit too forcefully. "I was just...watching a game, having a beer. That's all."

His lame excuse sounded flimsy even to my own ears. I leaned back, regarding him coolly. "If you're going to lie to me, Chase, you'll need to do better than that."

Leaning forward, I pinned him with an unwavering stare, determined to strip away every pretense left between us.

"Elena was murdered, Chase. And the police found evidence among her belongings directly linking her to me - my name and number. So unless you have an explanation for how a woman I've never met could have that, I think we both know exactly what role you played," I said.

Suffocating silence stretched between us. Chase's gaze skittered away as he struggled to respond.

Finally, he exhaled a mirthless chuckle, raking a hand through his hair. "I don't know why I'm surprised, honestly. You were always too perceptive."

Our eyes met again, his swimming with raw vulnerability. "You're right, Moxie. Elena...she was the other woman. The one I was seeing behind your back."

The frank admission deflated his bravado as his shoulders slumped. "I never meant for things to spiral so out of control. It started as a moment of weakness that turned into something more, something I couldn't extract myself from."

White-hot anger flared within me at his words, that searing betrayal rearing up again. "A moment of weakness?" I echoed, my voice trembling with barely restrained fury. "Is that what you call carrying on an entire affair, lying to me day after day while making me question my sanity?"

Chase flinched, his expression contorting in pain. "You're right, that's...that's a poor excuse, I know. What I did was unforgivable, and I can't make amends for the pain I caused you."

His eyes bored into mine, raw and imploring. "But you have to believe me, Mox - I never wanted anyone hurt. Especially not..." He shook his head slowly. "Not like this."

I searched his features, that treacherous longing to accept his words at face value warring with the cynicism that had become my armor against his deception. Could I trust anything he said, or would I invite another devastating betrayal?

Seeming to sense my struggle, Chase leaned forward, earnest. "Look, you and I...we have a history, for better or worse. As much as I've burned bridges between us, I need you to believe I'm telling the truth about Elena."

He paused, weighing his words carefully. "The thing is...she had been acting paranoid lately. Like she was sitting on some huge secret that could ruin lives if it got out."

My brow furrowed slightly. "What kind of secret?"

Chase shrugged helplessly. "Honestly, I don't know. She never gave details. But it was definitely related to our...relationship, if you could call it that."

A creeping sense of unease trickled down my spine as implications formed. If Elena uncovered something damning about their relation ship...

"You think she was trying to blackmail you," I stated flatly. "That's why she had my information - as leverage?"

A muscle ticked in Chase's jaw as he contemplated this. Finally, he inclined his head solemnly.

"It would explain a lot," he admitted. "Though I swear, I never intended for anything like this to happen."

The words lanced through me like shards of ice, resurrecting every bitter insecurity from his betrayal. My throat constricted as I struggled to maintain my composure and hard-won self-worth.

"Right, of course," I ground out. "Because that's always a reasonable justification for cheating and demolishing your partner's trust."

Chase had the decency to look abashed, though I could see the automatic defensiveness flickering - that ingrained reflex to deflect responsibility that had been his downfall.

Sensing this could escalate quickly, I cleared my throat and stood up. "Well, I think we've covered as much ground as we're going to for now. I need to get back before my grandmother wonders where I am."

Turning back to Chase, I felt my expression harden instinctively, that protective shell reflexively reasserting itself.

"I appreciate you...clarifying the details around Elena," I said, struggling to keep my voice level and professional. "But you need to understand - this changes nothing between us personally. You made your choices, and I've moved on."

The words felt laden with a tangle of lingering emotions I couldn't parse. Was I as resolved as I projected, or did I still cling to remnants of what we'd shared?

Chase seemed to read the conflicting undercurrents beneath my stony facade. His expression softened with naked longing bleeding through the cracks.

"I know, Mox," he said at last, tinged with regret. "Believe me, I know. And you're right - what I did is unforgivable. But...I hope you can let me try to make amends somehow. To be there for you during this mess, even if only as a source of information."

His words hung heavy with unspoken hopes and recriminations. Part of me ached to accept the olive branch, to let those protective walls crumble and that intimacy we'd shared rush back in.

But the wiser part, forged in the fires of his betrayal, knew better than to succumb. I was Moxie Rayburn. No matter what ghosts lurked, I would not be defined by them anymore.

Squaring my shoulders, I met Chase's soulful gaze with finality. "I'll be in touch if I need anything else related to the case," I stated, closing that door between us.

Then, without a backward glance, I turned and left. The bell tinkled cheerfully as I passed through the door, but I couldn't shake the disquieting sense that I'd just crossed a far more permanent threshold.

The drive back to the B&B was a whirlwind of confusion. As I replayed my conversation with Chase, part of me wanted to believe he was innocent. I thought I saw real vulnerability in his eyes. Yet, a cautious voice inside me warned against being naïve. How many times had his charm and excuses had fooled me, only to be hurt by his lies? Was this just another trick to win back my trust? Or was the remorse on his face genuine? Doubt flooded over me as I tightly gripped the steering wheel, leaving me unsure of what or whom to believe.

CHAPTER FIVE

Could I truly trust Chase's claims of innocence, or was this just another manipulation, another layer of deception? A part of me longed to believe the vulnerability I glimpsed in his eyes, to cling to the hope that the man I once loved wasn't capable of such darkness. Yet the wiser, more jaded part of me recoiled at the very notion.

With a weary sigh, I killed the engine and climbed out of my car. An older man had pulled up to the B&B at the same time. I assumed another guest.

"Hello," I said.

"You must be Moxie," he said, holding out his hand.

How had my reputation preceded me so quickly? "Yes, my grandmother, Iris, owns the Sunny Honey B&B."

He chuckled. "Yes, I know that. She called me over. I'm Arthur. Your grandmother and I go way back," he said, leading me to the front door.

"OK. Well, it's nice to meet you," I said. I was so ready for a nap. This night shift was really messing with my sleep schedule.

We entered the foyer, and he continued. "Iris said you could use an extra set of eyes on a delicate situation."

Of course she had. Iris Rayburn was nothing if not proactive. A pang of affectionate exasperation rippled through me as I regarded Arthur, taking in the faint whiff of his earthy cologne and the casual confidence in his bearing.

"I see," I said slowly, resuming my stride. "Well, I appreciate you coming, but I'm not entirely sure what she has filled you in on."

Arthur fell into step beside me, his hands tucked into the pockets of his well-worn khakis.

"Just the broad strokes -- some trouble with an old flame, and the possibility of a more...nefarious element at play."

I arched an inquisitive brow. Before I could sort through my thoughts, a warm, melodic voice drifted from the kitchen.

"Is that you, dear? I was starting to wonder--"

Grandma emerged from the adjoining room, her face alight with a radiant smile that faltered ever so slightly as her gaze landed on

Arthur. A fleeting expression I couldn't quite decipher flickered across her features before she smoothed it away, replacing it with a polite, if somewhat reserved, smile.

"Arthur," she greeted, her tone a careful blend of warmth and formality. "So glad you could make it."

The older man inclined his head respectfully.

"Iris," he replied, the simple utterance of her name carrying a weight of shared history that was not lost on me.

I watched the exchange with a mixture of curiosity and bewilderment, my earlier turmoil momentarily forgotten. There was an undeniable undercurrent between these two.

Clearing his throat, Arthur gestured vaguely between himself and Grandma.

"I certainly hope I can offer some...professional assistance," he said.

Grandma's features softened infinitesimally as she regarded the older man.

"I'm sure you can," she murmured, her gaze drifting briefly to me before returning to Arthur's weathered features. "Let's head into the kitchen."

We silently followed her and sat around the center island. Wordlessly, she put out a plate of cookies and put on a pot of coffee.

All at once, the weight of the past few days came crashing back down upon me with dizzying force. I exhaled shakily, struggling to maintain my composure even as my carefully constructed walls threatened to crumble under the onslaught of memories and turmoil.

Arthur started. "Why don't you tell me what's going on?"

I stared at him. If Grandma trusted him, I would do the same. I gave him the shortened version of why I ended back in Honeyridge Falls. And Grandma inserted the details of the visit by the detective.

"Are you OK?" Arthur asked, holding out his hand.

My voice sounded smaller than I would have liked. "I'm still...processing everything myself."

Grandma moved towards me as she reached out to grasp my hands.

"Oh, my sweet girl," she murmured, her voice thick with empathy. "I can only imagine the upheaval you're experiencing. But I really think Arthur can help."

Her gaze flicked towards Arthur once more.

Mustering a faint smile, I squeezed her hand gratefully, drawing strength from her steadfast presence.

"Eventually I'll be fine. How would you be able to help?" I asked Arthur.

He nodded thoughtfully, his gaze steady and reassuring. "Well, for starters, I can look into Chase's recent activities, see who he's been interacting with and where he's been. I also have some contacts in law enforcement who might provide us with a clearer picture of the investigation surrounding Elena's death."

I considered his words, the reality of the situation setting in. As much as I wanted to stay removed, the implications of Chase's potential involvement were too significant to ignore. "And if you find out he's involved?" I asked, the question hanging heavily between us.

Arthur's expression was grim. "Then we take that information to the police. But if he's innocent, I'll make sure the truth comes out. Either way, Moxie, I'm here to make sure this doesn't escalate further for you."

I nodded, feeling a mixture of relief and trepidation.

"Arthur, before you go, there's something else," Grandma said, her voice lower. "The detective mentioned finding Moxie's name and phone number in Elena's purse."

Arthur's eyebrows rose in surprise, and he turned back to me. "Is that so?" He paused, considering the implications. "Moxie, can you think of any reason Elena would have your contact details?"

I shook my head, bewildered. "No, I can't. I only now know her as the woman Chase was seeing behind my back."

He nodded slowly, jotting down something in his notebook. "Hmmm. I wonder why she might want to reach out to you for some reason."

The room was silent for a moment as the weight of his words sank in.

"Anything you can remember might help, even if it seems insignificant," Arthur added, his gaze intent on mine.

"I'll think it over," I promised, though my mind was already racing through past conversations with Chase, searching for a clue I might have missed.

"Good," he said. "I'll start with this new information first thing tomorrow."

As he left, the atmosphere in the room felt charged with a new urgency. Grandma and I exchanged a look, both of us troubled by the turn of events but grateful for Arthur's thorough approach.

"I didn't even know she had my number," I murmured, more to myself than to anyone else.

"We'll figure this out, dear," Grandma reassured me, her voice steady. "With Arthur helping, we're in excellent hands."

As Arthur reached for the doorknob to leave, he paused and turned back to face Grandma with a playful glint in his eyes. "Oh, and Iris," he began, his voice lowering to a more tender tone, "I nearly forgot to return this." From his pocket, he pulled out a small, intricately carved wooden spoon, its handle worn smooth by years of use. "You lent it to me last time I was here, for that peach cobbler we made together."

Her face lit up with a surprised and delighted smile. "Of course. I'd wondered where that had gone off to," she replied, taking the spoon from him. Her fingers brushed against his, lingering just a moment longer than necessary.

"There are still plenty of peaches in the orchard this year," Arthur added. "Maybe we could make another cobbler."

"I'd like that," Grandma said, her voice soft and wistful. "I'd like that very much."

Arthur nodded, his smile deepening as he finally turned to leave. The door closed gently behind him.

The air seemed to hum with unspoken words and lingering looks. I watched as she placed the wooden spoon back on a shelf, her fingers tracing the smooth grain of the wood. The small smile still played on her lips, and her eyes held a distant, dreamy quality.

Unable to resist, I nudged her playfully. "Grandma, if I didn't know better, I'd say there was a bit of a spark between you and Arthur."

Her cheeks tinged with pink, and she gave a light chuckle, shaking her head. "Oh, Moxie, you're imagining things. Arthur and I are just old friends, that's all."

"But that smile," I teased, leaning on the counter and enjoying the rare opportunity to see her flustered. "And that little spoon exchange? It was like something out of a romantic movie. Come on, admit it, there's something sweet there."

She continued to blush, but waved a dismissive hand, her smile betraying her words. "We have a lot of history, yes, and he's a dear friend. But that's all it is. Now, let's not get sidetracked. We have more pressing matters to think about."

Her attempt to steer the conversation away from her and Arthur only made me more curious, but I decided not to push her further. Instead, I smiled knowingly. "Alright, Grandma, if you say so. But I think it's wonderful, you know--having someone from the past who still makes you smile like that."

As we cleared the last of the cookies from the table, she turned the conversation towards a different topic. "So, tell me more about this storytelling event you're organizing. What's the plan?"

I perked up, grateful for the shift to something more creative and less fraught. "It's going to be an evening where local storytellers can share tales from Honeyridge Falls's past, maybe even some folklore and ghost stories. I want it to be a night that brings the community together."

"That sounds wonderful," she said, her eyes lighting up. "Let's work on the guest list."

"Yes, I'll need a lot of help with that. I'm not sure I know many people from being away for so long," I said.

She wiped the invisible crumbs from the counter, considering the options. "Well, I've got a few people in mind. First, there's Mr. Hawthorne, the high school history teacher. He's a treasure trove of local history and always has a new story to tell."

I nodded, writing the names.

"Then there's Linda Whitaker. She's not only a great storyteller, but she also knows all the family legends and ghost stories of Honeyridge Falls."

I laughed. "That will certainly add some spice to the evening. And, how about Arthur?" I added tentatively, watching her reaction.

She raised an eyebrow but smiled. "Arthur, huh? Well, he certainly has a way with words, and his years as a private investigator have given him more than a few intriguing stories to share."

"Yeah, I thought he could talk about some of the more mysterious aspects of Honeyridge Falls's past," I said, already picturing the event coming together.

"Now, what are you going to call this event? It needs a catchy name," she pointed out.

I nodded, having thought about a few options already. "I was thinking of something like 'Honeyridge Falls Haunts and Histories' to give it a bit of an alliterative appeal. Or maybe 'Tales from the Ridge' to keep it simple and inclusive."

"Both are good," she mused. "'Honeyridge Falls Haunts and Histories' has a nice ring to it, especially if Linda is going to delve into ghost stories. It sets the right tone for something a bit mysterious and intriguing."

I smiled, pleased with her feedback. "That's what I was hoping for."

She tapped her finger thoughtfully against her chin. "You know, you should really get Sammy involved," she suggested. "Having the event featured in the local newspaper would definitely help draw a bigger crowd."

I hesitated, the mere mention of Sammy causing a twinge of irritation.

"I know that look, Moxie," Grandma chuckled, reading my expression with ease. "But Sammy has the reach you need to make this event a success. She can get the word out better than anyone else in town."

I sighed, knowing she was right despite my reservations. "Yeah, you're probably right." Resigned but determined, I nodded. "Okay, I'll call her tomorrow. It's for the best, even if it means dealing with Sammy's... enthusiasm."

CHAPTER SIX

I blinked up at the ceiling, momentarily disoriented as the unfamiliar surroundings came into focus.

Right. The B&B. My new life in Honeyridge Falls.

With a groan, I rolled over and sat up, rubbing the lingering exhaustion from my eyes. My body felt weighted and sluggish after yet another late night manning the front desk. I was still adjusting to the nocturnal rhythms of the night shift, so different from my usual routine.

I shuffled to the window and pushed open the curtains. Down below, I could see Grandma tending to her beloved rose bushes that bordered the front porch.

As I turned from the window, my gaze landed on the photo collage Grandma had assembled for me, featuring snapshots from my childhood. Images of a grinning, gap-toothed ten-year-old me at the county fair, proudly clutching a blue ribbon for the pie I had entered. A timid sixteen-year-old me dressed up for prom, flanked by Grandma and Grandpa in the rose garden.

My fingers reached out, brushing over the frozen memories. So much had changed since then. I had changed. But being here made me feel that maybe, just maybe, I could find my way again.

After a quick shower and change of clothes, I headed downstairs, lured by the scents of sizzling bacon and brewing coffee. Grandma stood at the stove, humming softly while she tended to the cast-iron skillet. Two plates of fluffy eggs, crispy bacon, and buttery toast sat waiting on the kitchen island.

At the sound of my approach, she glanced up, her expression brightening. "Good morning! I thought I'd fix us up a hearty breakfast after your late night."

"You read my mind. This looks amazing," I said.

We carried our plates to the smaller round table nestled in the breakfast nook, settling in across from each other.

Finally, mouth still half-full of bacon, I met her gaze. "Thanks for making breakfast. You didn't have to go to the trouble, but I appreciate it."

She tutted, waving off my gratitude. "It was no trouble at all. I wanted to do something nice after your late night. Speaking of which, how did it go last night? Any issues I should know about?"

I took a sip of coffee, considering her question. "No major problems, thankfully. The night was pretty quiet. Oh, except around two in the morning, Mr. Newman called the front desk. He said his shower was making some clunking noises."

Grandma nodded knowingly. "That dang shower. I told Frankie he needed to take a look at the pipes." She sighed. "What did you do?"

"I went up and checked it out. I didn't see any immediate issues, but I made a note to have Frankie inspect it. Mr. Newman seemed fine with that." I hesitated, then added sheepishly, "I gave him one of the vouchers for a free breakfast though, just to smooth things over."

Chuckling, Grandma patted my hand. "You handled it perfectly. A little touch of hospitality can go a long way." Her expression grew thoughtful. "Anything else?"

I refilled my coffee as I recalled the rest of the uneventful night. "Let's see...around three-thirty, Ms. Edwards came down looking for extra blankets. Seems the heating in her room was a little wonky. I brought some up for her though, and she said that did the trick."

Grandma nodded approvingly. "Good thinking. I'll have someone look at that thermostat too. But I'm glad the night was relatively calm.

I remember my first few overnight shifts being quite the adjustment." She smiled sympathetically. "You'll get the hang of it soon enough."

A comfortable silence fell between us as we finished our meal. My thoughts drifted back to my talk with Chase.

Setting down my coffee mug, I asked, "Can I tell you something?" At her nod, I continued. "I've been thinking more about Chase a nd...everything. Honestly, it still hurts. I really did love him once." I exhaled heavily. "But the more distance I get, the more I'm realizing how unhealthy it had become. How I'd lost sight of myself."

She reached across the table, grasping my hand in her warm, re-assuring hold. "Oh sweetheart, you have such a big heart. I know it's painful, but you're also so strong. You'll come out of this even more sure of who you are."

I clung to her words, wanting so desperately to believe them. "I hope so. I just wish I hadn't ignored all the warning signs. Maybe if I'd walked away sooner, I could have avoided all this drama with...her." I couldn't bring myself to say Elena's name.

"We all wish we could change the past sometimes," Grandma said gently.

I felt my eyes well up from her unwavering faith in me. No matter how lost I felt, Grandma always reminded me of my strength. "Thank you," I whispered. "I'm still trying to find my footing, but knowing I have your support means everything."

She squeezed my hand. "You'll always have that, sweet girl. Now, what do you say we clear these dishes, then head over to Sweet Buzz? I'd love to see what they're setting up for the Honey Festival."

I readily agreed, the thought of fresh air and a change of scenery lifting my spirits. And it might just be an opportunity to secretly gather some clues. Within minutes, we had restored the kitchen to its usual tidy state. Linking her arm through mine, Grandma led me out the front door and to my car.

As we turned onto Clover Street, lined with charming cafes and local businesses, something caught my eye. Just up ahead stood Sweet Buzz Farms, the local honey producer that supplied many of the shops in town. Their trademark honeycomb signage adorned the exterior. Through the windows, I could see workers bustling around with industrious beehives.

A tinkling bell announced our arrival as Grandma and I stepped into the small gift shop. The quaint store was filled with the rich scents of beeswax and honey. One wall displayed neat rows of honey jars in shades ranging from pale golden to deep amber. Handmade soaps and candles, shaped like honeycombs, occupied another wall.

I was admiring a beautifully carved honey dipper when a voice called out.

"Iris Rayburn, is that you? Well, aren't you a sight for sore eyes!"

A plump, white-haired woman bustled around the counter to envelop Grandma in a warm embrace. Grandma's face lit up with delight.

"Rose! Oh, it's been far too long." She turned to me. "Moxie, you remember Rose Avery, don't you?"

I smiled as memories came flooding back. "Of course! Mrs. Avery, so nice to see you again." As a child, I'd spent many happy afternoons playing with Rose's granddaughter Lucy while our grandmothers sipped tea.

Just then, a pretty blonde woman around my age emerged from the back room carrying boxes. She put one of them down and raised her hand. "Hello, Mrs Rayburn."

"Hello, Tessa," Grandma said.

Turning back to Rose, Grandma said, "It's been a while since we've been here. If it's not too much trouble, could we get a tour and see what you're setting up for the Honey Festival?"

"Of course," said Rose, grabbing Grandma's hand. "Keith," Rose yelled into the back.

A tall, young man popped through the door from the back. "Yes?"

Rose smiled. "I'd love it if you could take a minute for the grand tour of our apiary for my good friend Iris and her granddaughter Moxie."

Keith saluted and led us through the door to the farm in the back.

The air was sweet with the scent of blooming wildflowers, mingling with the distinct musk of beeswax.

Keith, with an easy smile, explained the different types of hives and the roles within the bee colony. "Here we have the worker bees, the real heroes of our operation. They're the multitaskers: cleaners, nurses, builders, and foragers. Basically, they run the show."

Grandma chuckled, her eyes twinkling with curiosity. "And what about the queen bee? Still holding court?"

"Always," Keith replied with a grin. "She's the heart of the hive. Without her, all this," he gestured expansively, "wouldn't be possible."

I watched Grandma, struck by the youthful glow the visit brought to her face. "Looks like you have some competition, Grandma," I teased. "The queen bee might just be the most influential lady here."

She laughed, her gaze sweeping over the bustling hives. "Well, I suppose I can share the title. It's all about teamwork, right?"

Keith nodded, leading us further into the apiary. "Exactly! And speaking of teamwork, let's show you our new hybrid hives. They're designed to be more sustainable and bee-friendly."

As we continued through the apiary, the preparations for the Honey Festival were evident everywhere. Booths adorned with colorful banners lined a small clearing, each showcasing local honey, beekeeping tools, and crafts made from beeswax.

"Keith," Tessa called out, her voice carrying over the hum of activity, "we need you over by the crafts booth. There's a mix-up with the placements that needs sorting."

Keith turned towards her, nodding. "Got it, Tessa. I'll be right there."

As he excused himself, Tessa glanced at us, a polite smile briefly crossing her features. "I hope you're enjoying the tour. The festival's shaping up nicely, thanks to everyone's hard work."

"It looks amazing," I replied, genuinely impressed by the coordination all around us.

"Thank you," Tessa said, and followed Keith.

Grandma turned to me, her eyes still twinkling with the excitement of the tour. "Well, Moxie, that was invigorating! How about we head back and continue planning our storytelling event? I think today's visit might just spark some new ideas."

"Absolutely, Grandma," I replied

As she talked, my gaze wandered back to the workers. A tall figure had just entered the festival area, his blond hair visible beneath a baseball cap. My breath caught in my throat.

Chase.

I stood paralyzed, unable to tear my eyes away as he crossed over to one of the hives. What was he doing here? Chase had never expressed any interest in beekeeping before.

After exchanging a few words with the nearest worker, he lifted one of the boxes, peering at the honeycomb inside. Even from a distance, his face seemed more drawn and weary than I remembered.

"You okay, hun?" grandma asked.

Without a word, I pointed toward Chase.

Grandma's demeanor stiffened noticeably as she caught sight of Chase, a rare flash of irritation crossing her face. "Well, I never..." she muttered under her breath, then took a firm hold of my arm. "Moxie, let's not let anything spoil our day. We've got plenty to do."

Without waiting for my response, she gently but firmly guided me away from the scene. I glanced back once, catching a last glimpse of Chase, feeling a tangle of emotions at the sight of him.

What was he doing here?

CHAPTER SEVEN

The sight of Chase at the bee farm lingered in my mind. "Grandma, what do you think Chase was doing there? It just seemed so out of place for him, especially considering... you know, that Elena was killed there. It's such an awful coincidence."

She looked out the window, her gaze following the passing scenery, then turned to me in a more serious tone than usual. "It is troubling, Moxie. And honestly, it might not be just a coincidence. People often find themselves drawn back to the scene of their troubles, consciously or unconsciously. It's possible... Chase might be more involved than we'd like to believe."

"But beekeeping?" I questioned, still finding it hard to align this new image with the Chase I knew, especially under such grim circumstances. "He never showed any interest in things like that before. And to show up there, of all places--it's just... strange."

"Moxie," Grandma said gently, her voice pulling me back from the edge of my ruminations, "let's focus on the here and now. Our storytelling event is a chance to bring some good to the community and keep our minds occupied on positive things."

Her calm assurance and wise counsel helped steady the whirl of thoughts in my head. "You're right, Grandma. We'll focus on the event for now."

The drive back to the B&B passed in pensive silence. I kept replaying the moment in my mind, trying to make sense of his presence at the bee farm. Had it been mere coincidence, or was there something more to it?

We pulled up to the circular driveway and climbed out of the car. As we entered, a tall, slender man emerged from the staircase leading to the guest rooms. His tousled salt-and-pepper hair gave him a slightly disheveled air, and he wore a rumpled button-down shirt paired with khaki slacks. In one hand, he clutched a well-worn leather notebook.

"Good afternoon, ladies," he greeted us with a polite nod. His voice carried a faint rasp, like the gentle crackle of a fireplace.

Grandma offered him a warm smile. "Why, hello there, Mr. Moore. I trust you're settling in comfortably?"

So this was Jonathan Moore, the reclusive author who had booked one of our long-term suites. From what little Grandma had mentioned, he was an eccentric but well-respected writer working on his next novel.

"Please, call me Jonathan," he said, returning her smile. "And yes, your lovely establishment has been the perfect respite for my creative endeavors." His gaze shifted to me, and I felt the weight of his scrutiny. "You must be the granddaughter Iris has spoken of."

I extended my hand. "Moxie Rayburn. It's a pleasure to meet you, Jonathan."

His grip was firm as he shook my hand, his eyes studying me with an intensity that made me shift uncomfortably. "The pleasure is all mine, my dear. I must say, your grandmother did not do your beauty justice."

Heat crept into my cheeks at his bold compliment, and I quickly withdrew my hand. "You're too kind."

Grandma cleared her throat, shooting me an amused glance. "We were just returning from a visit to Sweet Buzz Farms. They're preparing for the annual Honey Festival."

Jonathan's eyebrows rose with interest. "Ah, yes, the bee farm. A fascinating place, I'm sure. Tell me, did you cross paths with anyone ...notable during your visit?"

There was an edge to his question that put me on alert. I exchanged a guarded look with Grandma before replying carefully, "We didn't interact with too many people, aside from a quick tour."

"I see." Jonathan's gaze remained fixed on me, as if silently urging me to elaborate.

When I remained silent, he pressed on. "And this festival, it's tied to the recent...unpleasantness in town, is it not?"

My heart skipped a beat. There was no mistaking what he was referring to -- Elena's murder. How much did this man know about the case?

Grandma spoke up, her tone clipped. "I'm afraid we don't have many details to share, Jonathan. It's an ongoing investigation."

He held up a placating hand. "Of course, of course. I meant no offense. Merely an idle curiosity, you understand. Curse of the trade." Despite his words, his expression remained keen, as if he were studying our every reaction.

An uncomfortable silence stretched between us, broken only by the chirping of birds in the nearby trees. Finally, Jonathan cleared his throat. "Well, I shan't keep you ladies any longer. In fact, I was just about to head over to the bee farm myself."

I blinked in surprise. "You were?"

He nodded, a faint smile playing at the corners of his mouth. "Indeed. As an author, I find it imperative to immerse myself in the settings and environments that inspire my writing. The sights, the sounds, the very essence of a place--all vital ingredients for crafting an authentic narrative."

"Yes," I replied, my curiosity piqued. "Actually, since you're visiting the bee farm and all, I have to ask--are your next book's events happening at a bee farm, too?"

He chuckled softly, the corners of his eyes crinkling with amusement. "Ah, Moxie, I would love to share more, but you know, a writer must keep some mystery in reserve until the book is available. It keeps the anticipation alive, both for the readers and for the writer himself. Let's just say, the natural world--and perhaps a farm of sorts--plays a crucial role in my next narrative adventure." He tipped his head in farewell. "Until we meet again, ladies. Enjoy your afternoon."

We watched as he strode out the door, his leather notebook tucked under his arm. Once he was out of sight, Grandma turned to me, her expression thoughtful.

"He's quite the character, isn't he?" she remarked, a hint of amusement in her voice.

I nodded slowly, but my mind was racing. "Yeah, he is. Did you notice how interested he was in the bee farm and Elena's murder? Almost like he knows more than he's letting on."

Grandma laughed softly, waving a dismissive hand. "Oh, Moxie, he's a writer. They're always curious and digging into things that might inspire their stories. It's probably nothing more than that."

I couldn't shake the unease creeping into my thoughts. "Maybe, but his sudden decision to visit the bee farm right after we mentioned it--it's more than a little coincidental."

"You're reading too much into it, dear," Grandma said, patting my arm reassuringly. "Writers need to immerse themselves in their settings to bring authenticity to their work. I think that's all it is."

I bit my lip, still unconvinced. "I guess. But there's something about him that doesn't quite add up."

Grandma smiled gently. "Let's not jump to conclusions. We'll keep an eye on things, but for now, let's give him the benefit of the doubt."

I nodded, though the weight of suspicion still settled over me like a heavy cloak.

Grandma glanced at her watch and sighed. "I need to prepare lunch for the guests. Can't have them going hungry, especially with all this excitement around." She gave me a quick hug before heading towards the kitchen. "I'll see you in a bit."

"Sure," I replied, my mind still on Jonathan.

With Grandma occupied, I retreated to the study, hoping some quiet time would help clear my thoughts. I sank into the armchair by the window, trying to shake off my lingering suspicions.

Just as I was relaxing, I heard a soft rustling sound. Looking up, I saw Sneaker. He hopped onto the desk with surprising grace, his green eyes fixing on me with an almost knowing look.

"Hey, Sneaker," I murmured, reaching out to scratch behind his ears.

He purred, leaning into my touch before settling down on a stack of papers, his tail flicking lazily. I couldn't help but smile at his antics, feeling a bit of the tension ease from my shoulders.

"You're a good listener, aren't you?" I said softly. "You think I'm being paranoid about Jonathan?"

He blinked slowly, as if considering my question. I chuckled, shaking my head. "Yeah, maybe you're right. But still, something doesn't sit right with me."

The shrill ringing of the desk phone jolted me from my reverie. I chuckled, wondering if Grandma would ever get with the 21st century technology. I snatched up the receiver, plastering on my best professional tone. "Sunny Honey Bed and Breakfast, this is Moxie speaking."

"Well, well, if it isn't little Miss Nancy Drew herself." The familiar snarky voice on the other end could belong to none other than Sammy.

I resisted the urge to groan. Of course she would catch wind of the storytelling event--Sammy had an uncanny ability to sniff out potential stories before anyone else.

"Hello, Sammy," I replied evenly. "To what do I owe the pleasure?"

"Cut the niceties, Rayburn," she scoffed. "You know why I'm calling. I need the full scoop on this storytelling shindig you and Granny Rayburn are cooking up."

I pinched the bridge of my nose, already feeling the beginnings of a headache. Dealing with her was always a delicate dance.

Still, I knew better than to rise to the bait. Taking a deep breath, I filled her in on the event details--the schedule, featured speakers, and planned activities. To her credit, Sammy remained mostly silent, save for the occasional hum of acknowledgment.

When I finished, she let out a low whistle. "Not too shabby, Mox. Might actually be worth a blurb in the Nectar News."

I bristled at her patronizing tone. "Gee, thanks for the ringing endorsement."

"Hey, I call 'em like I see 'em," she retorted. "But don't worry, I'll give it the old Sammy spin. You know how I do."

I cringed at the thought of Sammy's tendency to embellish and sensationalize. "Just try to stick to the facts this time, okay? No need to exaggerate or editorialize."

She let out an exaggerated sigh. "Fine, fine. I'll be a model of journalistic integrity, scout's honor." The sarcasm in her voice suggested otherwise, but I knew better than to argue further.

"I'll send over the press release later," I said, eager to end the conversation. "But please, Sammy, try to keep it accurate this time."

"Yeah, yeah, I got it," she grumbled. "No need to nag. Later, Rayburn."

The line went dead, leaving me staring at the receiver in exasperation.

Shaking my head, I returned the phone to its cradle and leaned back in my chair, letting out a weary sigh.

CHAPTER EIGHT

I looked up from the front desk, where I'd been organizing the latest guest check-ins.

"Arthur," I greeted him with a smile that masked my inner turmoil. "What brings you here?"

He returned my smile with a nod, his eyes twinkling with a hint of mischief. "Thought I'd drop by and see if you'd be interested in a little field trip."

I raised an eyebrow, intrigued. "A field trip? Where to?"

"Bumble Brews," he replied, leaning casually against the counter. "I have a hunch some of the bee farm workers might be there after their shift. Could be an excellent opportunity to gather some intel."

I glanced at the clock. My night shift was starting soon, but the lure of potential clues was too tempting to resist. "Give me a minute to let Grandma know."

His eyes softened. "Take your time."

After a quick conversation with Grandma, who assured me she could handle things for a couple of hours, I grabbed my coat and joined Arthur outside.

As we drove to Bumble Brews, Arthur filled me in on the latest from his law enforcement contacts. "Unfortunately, no new leads from the police about Elena's murder," he said, frustration in his voice. "But sometimes, you learn more from the people around a situation than from the official reports."

I nodded, appreciating his seasoned insight. "Let's hope tonight is one of those times."

The neon sign above Bumble Brews flickered in the twilight, casting an intermittent glow over the entrance. Arthur and I approached the weathered wooden door, the sounds of laughter and clinking glasses drifting out from within.

"You ready for this?" he asked, his voice low.

I took a steadying breath, nodding firmly. "Let's do it."

He pushed open the door, and we stepped inside, the warm, amber-tinged atmosphere of the bar enveloping us. The air was thick with the mingled scents of beer, pretzels, and an undercurrent of smoke from the fireplace crackling in the corner.

I scanned the room, taking in the clusters of patrons scattered around the high-top tables and the long, polished bar that stretched along the back wall. My gaze landed on a group huddled in one of the booths, their laughter carrying above the general din.

"There," I murmured, nudging Arthur's arm. "I recognize a few of them from the bee farm."

He followed my line of sight, his expression hardening ever so slightly. "Good eye. Let's find a spot where we can keep an eye on them."

We wove our way through the crowd, eventually settling at a table tucked against the wall, with a clear view of the bee farm workers' booth. Arthur signaled the server, ordering us a couple of beers to maintain our cover.

As we waited for our drinks, I studied the group more closely. Keith, one of the younger workers, was animatedly recounting some story, his hands gesturing wildly as his colleagues listened with rapt attention. Beside him sat Tessa, her blonde hair pulled back in a messy ponytail, her expression one of amused exasperation.

Keith's laughter rose above the background hum of Bumble Brews as he leaned closer to his audience, his eyes twinkling with mischief.

"And then, believe it or not, he turns to me and says, 'That's not how you handle a queen bee, son!' Can you imagine? Me, getting schooled on bee-handling by a tourist in Bermuda shorts and a bucket hat!"

The table erupted into laughter, the warm glow of camaraderie washing over the group. Tessa rolled her eyes playfully, nudging Keith gently with her elbow. "Oh, come off it. You're just sore because he turned out to know more about bees than you do!"

Keith feigned a wounded look, clutching his heart. "You wound me, Tessa. Here I am, sharing my trauma, and you mock my pain."

As the laughter continued, another girl at the table, who had been quietly sipping her drink, leaned forward with a smirk. "Don't let them rile you up, Keith. We all know you're the bee whisperer around here. Besides, those Bermuda shorts were the real crime."

Her interjection drew another round of laughter. Even Keith couldn't help but grin. Tessa nodded. "Exactly, and thank goodness you were there to save the day, Melissa, fashion police and bee expert all in one."

The server returned with our beers, and we settled in, nursing our drinks while keeping a watchful eye on the group. For a while, their conversation seemed to revolve around work and the upcoming Honey Festival, nothing out of the ordinary.

Then Keith mentioned a name that made my heart skip a beat --
Chase.

I leaned forward, straining to catch the snippet of conversation, but a sudden burst of raucous laughter from the bar drowned their words out.

Frustration churned within me as I realized I had missed whatever they said about my ex-boyfriend. Had it been something innocuous, or was there more to it?

Arthur must have sensed my agitation, for he reached across the table and gave my hand a reassuring squeeze. "Easy there, Moxie. We might not catch everything, but we'll keep listening."

I exhaled slowly, nodding in agreement. As much as I wanted answers, I knew rushing to conclusions would only lead us astray.

As the night wore on, the bar emptied, the lively chatter dwindling to a low murmur. Finally, the group we had been observing rose from their booth, gathering their belongings and heading for the exit.

Arthur drained the last of his beer, setting the empty glass down with a hollow thunk. "Well, that was a bust."

I slumped back in my chair, deflated. "Yeah, I was really hoping we'd pick up on something useful."

He shrugged, his expression inscrutable. "Can't win 'em all, kid. At least we tried."

As we made our way out of Bumble Brews and headed toward his car, I hesitated before climbing into the passenger seat, the evening air cool against my skin. Arthur noticed my pause, tilting his head slightly in question.

"Arthur," I started, my voice low, the hum of the departing crowd fading behind us. "There's something else. Today, I went to the bee farm." I gulped. "I... I saw Chase there. He's working at the farm now."

Arthur's expression tensed as he opened the driver's door, pausing to take in my words. "Chase? Your ex?" He frowned, his eyes meeting mine under the streetlight's glow. "You didn't know he was involved there?"

I shook my head, climbing into the car as he held the door for me. "No, I had no idea. It caught me off guard. And now, hearing his name tonight... It makes me wonder if he could actually be involved in Elena's murder."

Arthur slid into the driver's seat, inserting the key into the ignition but not turning it. He turned to face me, his features drawn in the dim light. "This complicates things," he admitted, his voice low. "If he is involved, things could get dangerous for you. We need to be extra careful."

I nodded, the gravity of the situation settling in. "I know. It's just a lot to take in. I thought I was over him, but seeing him there, and now this... It's just too much."

Arthur reached out, placing a reassuring hand on my shoulder. "We'll figure this out, Moxie. One step at a time. For now, let's get you home and we can plan our next move."

With a heavy sigh, I leaned back against the seat, the car's engine starting with a soft rumble, carrying us away into the night.

Inside, the antique lamps lining the walls bathed the foyer in a soft glow.

Creaking footsteps on the staircase drew my attention, and I looked up to see Grandma descending, a concerned expression etched onto her features.

"There you are, Moxie," she said, her voice a gentle admonishment. "I was starting to worry."

I offered her an apologetic smile, suddenly feeling like a scolded child. "Sorry, Grandma. We were trying to get any details we could."

Her brow furrowed as she studied my face, no doubt picking up on the tension that still lingered within me. "I see. And did this stakeout prove fruitful?"

I shook my head, sinking onto the plush settee that adorned the foyer. "Not really."

A contemplative silence stretched between us, punctuated only by the soft ticking of the grandfather clock in the corner. Finally, Grandma spoke up, her voice gentle but laced with wisdom.

"You know, Moxie, sometimes the hardest lessons in life are about learning to let go." She gave my hand another tender squeeze. "As much as you want to solve this mystery, you can't let it consume you. There's more to life than chasing after answers that might never come."

I opened my mouth to protest, but she held up a hand, effectively silencing me.

"Now, now, hear me out. I'm not saying you should give up entirely. But perhaps it's time to take a step back, let the professionals handle things for a while." She offered me a warm smile, her eyes shining with affection.

Just as we were settling into the comforting calm of our conversation, the front door burst open with a clatter that jolted us both. Jonathan stormed into the lobby, his hair disheveled and his coat half-buttoned, carrying the chaotic energy of a windstorm.

"Iris, Moxie, you won't believe it!" he exclaimed breathlessly, his eyes wide with an intense gleam of excitement. He barely paused to catch his breath, waving a stack of hastily scribbled notes in the air. "I went to the bee farm today--so much inspiration, so many details for my novel! It's all coming together now!"

Without waiting for a response, he bounded towards the stairs, taking two at a time. "I have to write this down before I forget!" he called over his shoulder, disappearing up the staircase with a thud of hurried footsteps.

Grandma and I exchanged bewildered looks, her eyebrows raised in silent question. I shrugged helplessly, still processing the whirlwind that was Jonathan.

"He seems... inspired," I finally managed, the understatement hanging between us as we listened to the distant sound of Jonathan rummaging through his room upstairs.

Grandma nodded, a hint of amusement softening her worried features. "Indeed. Though I'm not sure what to make of it all." She sighed, smoothing the front of her cardigan. "Let's just hope his sudden burst of creativity doesn't keep the entire house awake tonight."

"You know, Grandma," I said, hesitating as I weighed my words, "it's great that Jonathan's found so much inspiration, but don't you think his interest in the bee farm seems a bit... intense? It's just a place for beekeeping, after all."

Grandma paused, her expression turning thoughtful. "You have a point."

I nodded, folding my arms as I leaned back. "Yeah, and with every-thing going on--Chase working there and all the troubles--it makes me wonder why he's so drawn to it. I mean, what if there's something more he's stumbled upon?"

Chapter Nine

I wandered through the bustling activity, taking in the sight of half-assembled booths and the hum of conversation. The air was thick with the scent of flowers and honey, blending into a comforting aroma. As I walked, I noticed a woman struggling with an enormous banner, trying to secure it to a booth frame.

"Do you need some help?" I called out, stepping closer.

She turned, a look of mild surprise on her face. "Oh, that would be great! Thanks," she replied, her voice warm and inviting. Her blonde hair was tied back in a messy ponytail, and her bright smile lit up her features.

I held the banner in place while she secured it, introducing myself. "I'm Moxie, by the way."

"Nice to meet you, Moxie. I'm Karen," she said, extending a hand once the banner was fixed. "Are you here for the festival?"

"Actually, I'm here to volunteer and get a feel for the place," I explained, sipping my coffee. "I figured it might help with some things I'm working on."

Karen's eyes sparkled with curiosity. "Well, you're in the right place. We can always use an extra set of hands. Follow me. I'll show you around and get you started."

As we walked, Karen pointed out various booths and areas of the farm, sharing little anecdotes and bits of history. "This festival has been a big part of our community for years," she said with pride. "Everyone comes together to make it a success."

I nodded, appreciating her enthusiasm. "It sounds wonderful. I'm glad I can help."

Karen's expression softened as she led me towards a quieter section of the farm. "Ever since Elena's... incident, things have been somber around here," she admitted, a hint of sadness in her voice.

I placed a gentle hand on her arm, offering what comfort I could. "I'm so sorry about your friend. That must have been devastating."

She nodded, blinking back tears. "It was. Elena and I had been best friends since we were kids, you know? We grew up together on this farm, learned everything about beekeeping side by side." A melancholic smile tugged at the corners of her mouth. "She was always the brave one, never afraid to shake things up or speak her mind."

I tilted my head, curiosity piqued. "What do you mean?"

Karen hesitated, chewing her lip as if debating how much to share. Finally, she exhaled, her shoulders slumping. "A few weeks before she died, Elena started acting... different. Secretive. She'd disappear for hours at a time, claiming she was working on some special project for the festival."

My ears perked up at the mention of a potential lead. "Did she ever tell you what this project was?"

Karen shook her head, her brow furrowed. "Not really. Whenever I asked, she'd just get this mischievous glint in her eye and say, 'You'll see soon enough.' I figured she was just trying to surprise me, you know? Plan some grand unveiling or something."

A lump formed in my throat as I considered the tragic implications of her words. "But then she never got the chance."

Karen's eyes glistened with unshed tears. "No. Whatever she was working on, it died with her that night." She sniffed, swiping at her cheeks with the back of her hand. "I can't help but wonder if maybe, just maybe, that secret project of hers had something to do with her murder."

Before I could respond, a deep voice cut through our somber conversation. "Karen? Everything okay over here?"

We turned to see a tall, broad-shouldered man approaching, concern etched into his ruggedly handsome features.

Karen offered him a watery smile, gesturing towards me. "Yeah, Adam, we're fine. This is Moxie. She's volunteering with us for the festival."

The man studied me for a moment before extending his hand. "Nice to meet you, Moxie. I'm Adam."

I shook his hand, noticing the strength of his grip. "Nice to meet you too, Adam."

He held my gaze, a curious look in his eyes. "Your name sounds familiar. Have we met before?"

I shook my head, though a feeling of unease tugged at me. "I don't think so. I've just returned to town after being gone for several years. I'm the new night clerk at my grandma's B&B."

Adam nodded slowly, his expression thoughtful. "Well, welcome. We can definitely use the help."

As he walked away, I couldn't shake the feeling that there was more to his familiarity with my name.

Karen leaned closer, her voice low. "That's Elena's ex-boyfriend. They've had a complicated history."

A knot twisted in my stomach as I absorbed this information. "I see," I murmured, glancing back at Adam's retreating figure. The parallels between his situation and mine were unsettling, but it also made me wonder if I had just found a potential additional suspect.

Karen gave me a sympathetic look. "It's been tough on him, and on all of us."

As the afternoon wore on, the festival grounds took shape, vibrant booths and colorful banners lining the pathways. Karen and I stepped back to admire our handiwork, wiping the sweat from our brows.

"Not too shabby, huh?" she grinned, her eyes sparkling with pride.

I nodded, unable to suppress a smile of my own. "It's really coming together. You guys have outdone yourselves."

A commotion at the far end of the field caught our attention, and we turned to see a group of workers clustered around the main stage, their voices raised in agitated tones. Frowning, Karen gestured for me to follow as we made our way over to investigate.

As we approached, the cause of the disturbance became clear: one of the support beams for the stage had buckled, causing a section of the platform to collapse in on itself. Workers scrambled to assess the damage, their expressions ranging from concern to outright panic.

"What in the world happened here?" Karen demanded, her hands planted firmly on her hips as she surveyed the wreckage.

A young man I recognized as Keith stepped forward, his face pale and drawn. "We're not sure. One minute we were securing the last few bolts, and the next thing we knew, the whole thing just gave way."

Could this be more than just an accident? There seemed to be a number of secrets at the bee farm.

As if sensing my train of thought, Karen leaned in close, her voice low. "You don't think..."

Before she could finish her question, a muffled groan emanated from beneath the rubble, effectively silencing the crowd. We watched in horror as a pair of dusty work boots emerged, followed by a dazed and bloodied face.

"Someone call an ambulance!" Karen shouted, her voice laced with panic. "And get the foreman over here, now!"

The ensuing chaos was a blur of activity, with workers rushing to assist the injured man and secure the area. Through the commotion, I caught snatches of hushed whispers, words laced with fear and accusation.

"...never should have come back..."

"...asking for trouble, poking around like that..."

"...think they know something?"

As the paramedics arrived and whisked away the injured worker, a familiar figure pushed his way through the crowd, his expression thunderous. Detective Wilson surveyed the scene, his gaze sweeping over the wreckage and the gathered onlookers.

Sure enough, as the commotion died down, he made a beeline for me, his jaw set in a grim line. I steeled myself, squaring my shoulders to prepare for the confrontation.

"Ms. Rayburn," he greeted me, his tone clipped and professional. "What are you doing here?"

I hesitated, searching for a plausible excuse. "Oh, just volunteering for the festival, trying to help and...you know, get involved in local activities."

He narrowed his eyes, clearly not buying my vague explanation. "Cut the nonsense, Moxie. You're investigating, aren't you?"

Caught, I sighed, my shoulders slumping. "Yes, I am. But I think I might be onto something--"

He cut me off with a stern look. "Leave it to the professionals. We don't need civilians interfering, especially now."

"But Detective," I protested, "if you'd just listen--"

"No buts," he said, his voice hardening. "This is serious business, Moxie. People could get hurt if you keep sticking your nose where it doesn't belong. We're closing in on a suspect, and I don't need you complicating things." He stomped away.

His words hit me like a slap in the face, the weight of his warning sinking in. Was Chase going to be arrested?

Even as the rational part of my mind acknowledged the truth in his words, a deeper, more stubborn part refused to back down. There was something bigger at play here, something that had already claimed one life, and I couldn't shake the feeling that uncovering the truth was the only way to prevent further tragedy.

Footsteps crunched on the gravel behind me, and I turned to see Karen approaching, her expression etched with concern.

"You okay, Moxie?" she asked, her voice gentle. "That was... a lot to take in today."

I sighed, running a hand through my tousled hair. "Yeah, you could say that again." I hesitated as I debated whether to voice the thoughts swirling in my mind.

Karen seemed to sense my internal struggle, offering me an understanding smile. "You know, Elena always used to say that the bees could sense when something was off in the hive. Like they had this intuition, this sixth sense for danger."

I quirked an eyebrow, intrigued by the metaphor.

"Thank you so much for your help today," Karen said. "I'm sorry it was so dramatic." She gestured toward the wreckage.

"I'm just glad nobody was hurt worse," I said.

I walked to my car, piecing together the details of my day, replaying the conversation with the detective. Was there anything he said that would give me insight who might be arrested?

As I drove back to the B&B, I felt a nagging sense of unease. Despite my better judgment, I called Chase.

Taking a deep breath, I hit the speed dial and listened to the phone ring. On the third ring, he picked up, sounding unusually cheerful.

"Moxie? Hey, it's great to hear from you!" His voice was warm and eager, a stark contrast to my own apprehensive tone.

"Hi Chase," I replied, keeping my voice cool and distant. "I just left Sweet Buzz Farms and needed to check in with you about something."

There was a slight pause before he spoke again, his tone tinged with concern. "Sure, anything. What's going on?"

"Do you know much about Adam?" I asked directly.

"Adam?" Chase's voice tightened a bit. "Yeah, he's Elena's ex-boyfriend. Why do you ask?"

I took a moment, then pressed on. "Do you think Adam could have had anything to do with Elena's death?"

Chase's surprise was obvious. "You think Adam killed Elena?"

"I don't know," I admitted, gripping the steering wheel tighter. "Detective Wilson told me they're close to arresting a suspect. I just... I have a feeling there's more to this story."

There was a pause on the other end of the line before he responded, his voice filled with hopeful excitement. "If the detective thinks Adam is the killer, and he's going to be arrested, that would be a relief."

"Yeah, it would be," I replied, trying to keep my thoughts in check. "We'll see what happens."

"Thanks for letting me know," he said.

I paused, unsure if I should venture further into the investigation. I gripped the steering wheel.

"Mox?" Chase said. "You still there?"

I blew out my breath. "Yes. So, Chase," I started, skeptical whether I would hear the truth. "Are you working at Sweet Buzz Farms?"

"Um, why do you ask?" he said.

"I saw you the other day when Grandma and I were there," I said.

"Yeah. I'm kind of embarrassed, but I need money," he replied.

Was that just a cover for something deeper? Though, he hadn't managed money well when we were together. Always opting for expensive things beyond his means.

"Be careful, okay?" he added.

"I will. Take care, Chase," I said and hung up.

Part of me hoped that Adam might be the killer, bringing some closure to the chaos. And closure to my relationship with Chase.

Chapter Ten

The kitchen hummed with activity as Grandma and I put the final touches on the preparations for the storytelling event.

"Moxie, can you pass me the chamomile blend?" she asked, her eyes sparkling with excitement. "It will pair nicely with the lavender honey biscuits."

"Sure thing," I replied, reaching for the jar labeled "Chamomile Dream." I couldn't help but smile at her enthusiasm.

"We need a good variety of teas," she continued. "Guests love having options."

"We should include the green tea with jasmine," I suggested, arranging the jars neatly. "I think it'll be a hit."

"Good idea." She paused, a nostalgic smile playing on her lips. "I'm so glad we're starting up this tradition again. Your grandpa and I started them to bring the community together. There's something magical about sharing stories over a cup of tea."

I loved hearing her stories about the B&B's history. "Do you have a favorite memory from the events?" I asked.

Her eyes twinkled. "One of my favorites is when old Mr. Thompson tried to tell a ghost story and got so scared he couldn't finish. The children had to comfort him instead of the other way around."

We both laughed, the sound filling the cozy kitchen. It felt good to share this moment of lightness amidst the tension of the ongoing investigation.

"Let's move on to the decorations," Grandma said, her tone more businesslike. "We need to make sure everything looks just right for this first event tomorrow."

We entered the great room where we planned to host the guests. I opened a box of fairy lights, their soft glow adding a magical touch to the room. "I think these will look great draped along the mantel," I said, unwinding the string.

"Absolutely," she agreed, spreading out vintage tablecloths with delicate lace edges. "These tablecloths have been in the family for generations."

I helped her smooth out the fabric, admiring the intricate patterns. "They're beautiful, Grandma. It's like stepping back in time."

Next, we turned our attention to the centerpieces. Grandma had gathered jars and vases filled with wildflowers from the surrounding fields. The vibrant colors and sweet scents brought a bit of the outdoors inside, adding to the B&B's rustic charm.

As we stepped back to admire our handiwork, she sighed contentedly. "It's perfect, Moxie. Just like old times."

I nodded, pride swelling in my chest. "It really is. I think our guests are going to love it."

From the corner of my eye, I noticed Jonathan slipping out the front door. His sudden departure piqued my curiosity, and a knot of suspicion formed in my stomach.

"Grandma, I just remembered I need to take Jonathan more towels," I said, excusing myself from the preparations.

She nodded, her focus still on the arrangements. "Sounds good. I think we're done here for now."

As I ascended the stairs, my mind raced with possibilities. Jonathan's odd behavior and his interest in the bee farm were too coincidental to ignore.

Reaching the second floor, I hesitated for a moment outside his door, then knocked lightly. When there was no answer, I took a deep breath and pushed the door open, using the pretext of delivering fresh towels to justify my intrusion if someone happened by.

The room was neat, almost too neat, with everything meticulously in place. I immediately noticed a stack of papers on the desk, with the top sheet displaying the title of a manuscript. I quickly dropped the towels on the bathroom counter.

Heart pounding, I moved closer and picked up the top pages. The story unfolded before me, and with each paragraph, my unease grew. With eerie precision, the plot of the manuscript mirrored the real-life events at the bee farm. The fictional murder involved a staged bee swarm attack--a gruesome detail that made my skin crawl.

I flipped through more pages, my hands trembling. The detective character in the manuscript theorized about the involvement of a close associate of the victim, drawing a suspicious parallel to Chase. The similarities were too strong to be mere coincidence.

As I read further, my eyes landed on a passage detailing the victim's last moments. The chillingly vivid description matched the scene I had seen in my nightmares. My pulse quickened, and a sense of dread settled over me. Could Jonathan be involved in Elena's murder, or was he just an uncanny predictor of tragic events?

I slipped out of the room as quietly as possible, my mind still reeling from what I had discovered. The corridor was empty, and I breathed a sigh of relief.

Leaning against the wall, I pulled out my phone. Closing my eyes, I waited for Arthur to answer. There had to be more progress. The suspense was killing me.

"Moxie, what's going on?" he asked, his voice calm and reassuring.

"I found something in Jonathan Moore's room," I said, my voice barely above a whisper. "His manuscript... it's about a murder at a bee farm."

There was a brief pause on the other end of the line. "What do you mean?"

I quickly summarized the key points of Jonathan's story: the victim found in a storage shed, the staged bee swarm attack, the mysterious notes.

"Arthur, it's like he's writing a fictionalized version of what happened to Elena," I continued, my voice growing more frantic. "Do you think he could be involved?"

Arthur sighed, his tone thoughtful. "Moxie, I know Jonathan's work well. He has a penchant for dramatic twists and intricate plots. It's possible that what you found is just a bizarre coincidence."

"But the details are so specific," I insisted, gripping the phone tighter. "It's too much to be just a coincidence."

"I understand your concern," Arthur said gently. "But let's not jump to conclusions. Jonathan is a talented writer, and his narrative style often includes elements of suspense and misdirection. It's what makes his work so compelling."

I paced behind the reservation desk, my mind churning. "So you think he just happened to write a story about a bee farm murder that just occurred?"

"It's not impossible," Arthur replied. "Writers often draw inspiration from real-life events, sometimes without even realizing it. It's a way to process and explore different scenarios. But that doesn't mean he's directly involved in the crime."

I had to trust Arthur, his professional expertise. To my novice brain, Jonathan was all kinds of guilty. But maybe I let my desperation to help Chase get off the hook cloud my judgment.

"Besides, those details differ from the crime," he said. "I was able to finagle some details from my friend on the force."

I dropped into the desk chair and grabbed a paper and pencil. "That's great. Do tell."

He cleared his throat. I heard paper rustling. "The murder took place at the bee farm during the preparations for the Honey Festival. Specifically, it happened inside a secluded storage shed used for beekeeping equipment. The time of the murder was late evening, just after most workers had left, but while some were still preparing for the next day's festival activities."

I scribbled furiously, trying to capture every detail. "Okay, and what about the weapon?"

"A beekeeping tool," Arthur replied. "Specifically, a hive tool used for prying apart hive boxes. It was found next to Elena's body, but the fingerprints had been wiped clean. She died from blunt force trauma to the back of the head, suggesting a surprise attack from behind."

A chill ran down my spine as I wrote. "And who found her?"

"A fellow bee farm worker," Arthur continued. "He went to retrieve more supplies from the shed late in the evening and stumbled upon Elena's body."

I paused, absorbing the information. "So it was a beekeeping tool. That fits with the setting. But the hive tool... it's such a specific weapon."

"Yes," Arthur agreed. "And it shows that the killer was familiar with beekeeping equipment. They knew what tool to use and how to use it to inflict fatal damage."

"Did the worker see anyone suspicious?" I asked, hoping for a lead.

"Unfortunately, no," Arthur said. "He was too shocked to notice anything out of the ordinary. By the time he called for help, anyone who might have been around could have easily slipped away."

I sighed, feeling the weight of the investigation pressing down on me. "This still doesn't clear Chase. I'm guessing since he works at the farm, he's familiar with some of this stuff."

Arthur's voice softened. "I know, Moxie. But we can't jump to conclusions. We need more evidence. The details from Jonathan's manuscript might be coincidental, but they could also provide a fresh perspective. We need to consider all angles."

"Thanks, Arthur. I really appreciate it," I said, feeling a bit of the weight lifted from my shoulders.

"Anytime. Keep me posted on any new developments," he replied.

I stood there for a moment, taking a deep breath and trying to clear my head. Arthur's words had helped to ground me, but the manuscript still nagged at the back of my mind. I knew I had to stay vigilant and keep looking for answers.

Just then, Grandma came downstairs with Sneaker cradled in her arms. The cat was howling softly, his ears flat against his head.

"What's wrong with Sneaker?" I asked, concern lacing my voice.

Grandma frowned, her eyes full of worry. "I found him in Jonathan's room, howling and scratching at the door. I wonder how he got in there."

A pang of guilt struck me. I had entered Jonathan's room under the pretense of delivering towels, and now Sneaker had been found there too. I needed to be more careful. Taking a deep breath, I decided it was time to come clean.

"Grandma, there's something I need to tell you," I began, my voice wavering slightly. "I've been feeding Sneaker. Although I should have asked first, he seemed so hungry and lonely that I couldn't ignore him. I didn't mean to cause any trouble."

Her expression softened, but there was still a hint of disapproval in her eyes. "Moxie, you should have told me. Sneaker's been getting into places he shouldn't be, and we need to be careful with our guests' privacy."

"I know, and I'm really sorry," I said earnestly. "I'll take full responsibility for Sneaker. I'll make sure he doesn't cause any more problems. Can he stay, please?"

Grandma sighed, her gaze shifting to the still-howling cat. After a moment, she nodded. "Alright, Moxie. Sneaker can stay, but you need to keep a close eye on him. Make sure he doesn't disturb any of the guests."

A wave of relief washed over me, and I couldn't help but smile. "Thank you, Grandma. I promise I'll take good care of him."

With Sneaker in my arms, I headed up to my room. The weight of the investigation still pressed heavily on me, but for now, I allowed myself a moment of peace. Sneaker curled up beside me as I lay down, his purring a soothing lullaby. I closed my eyes, determined to catch a quick nap before my shift started.

CHAPTER ELEVEN

As the early guests settled into the cozy embrace of the great room, I glanced at the antique clock perched above the mantel, noting the absence of a few key attendees. The flutter of excitement in my stomach mixed with a hint of concern. Grandma noticed my distracted gaze.

"Is everyone here yet?" she asked, smoothing down her apron.

I shook my head. "Still waiting on a few more. I'll call them just to make sure they're on their way." Pulling out my phone, I stepped into the quiet of the hallway.

The first call went to Mrs. Richmond, known for her punctuality. When she answered, her voice was apologetic. "Oh, dear, I thought it was tomorrow evening! The newspaper said the 15th, didn't it? I'm so sorry, Moxie."

Confusion creased my brow. "No, it was supposed to be today, the 14th." A sinking feeling formed as I ended the call with a promise from Mrs. Richmond to hurry over.

Next, I called Leonard Griffith, who echoed the same mistake. "I'm terribly sorry, Moxie. I've mixed up the dates from the press release. Give me fifteen minutes; I'll be there." I hadn't seen him leave the B&B, so I assumed he would be here.

I returned to the great room where Grandma was chatting with Arthur, trying to maintain the cheerful atmosphere despite the half-filled room. As I approached, she looked up, a question in her eyes.

"We've had a minor hiccup," I explained. "There's been a date mix-up in the press release Sammy sent out. A few people thought it was tomorrow."

Grandma frowned, then her expression softened. "Well, we'll just have to adjust. It's important that everyone who wants to be here can make it. We can use the extra time to make sure everything is perfect."

Nodding, I appreciated her ever-adaptable nature. "Thank you. I'll let everyone know we're starting a bit late."

As I walked back to the group, my phone buzzed with messages from the delayed guests promising their quick arrival.

I quickly scanned the on-line press release. Sure enough. It was wrong. Was that deliberate? Why would Sammy do that? I wanted to assume good intent. But it was Sammy.

It wasn't long before our delayed guests arrived. I put my hand over my heart, attempting to quell the racing. This first event was so important to me that it went well.

I couldn't wait to hear their stories. I already knew that we had to have these sessions regularly. Having these sessions on a regular basis would be a treasured way to keep our history.

I spotted Arthur chatting amiably with Grandma. He caught my eye and gave me a warm smile and a subtle nod. I was sure there was something more going on between those two, but time would tell.

Once everyone had settled in with cups of steaming tea and plates of honey-drizzled pastries, Grandma took the floor, her warm presence commanding the room's attention.

"Welcome, friends, to the first Sunny Honey B&B storytelling evening in many years," she began, her voice rich with emotion. "Tonight, we celebrate the power of shared stories, the legends and histories that have woven together to create the vibrant tapestry that is our beloved Honeyridge Falls."

A hush fell over the room as she continued, "We have gathered some of our town's finest storytellers, each with their own unique perspective and tales to share. So sit back, sip your tea, and let the magic of storytelling transport you."

With a gracious gesture, Grandma invited Edward Hawthorne to take the floor. The history teacher rose, his movements polished and confident, and began to weave a captivating tale of Honeyridge Falls' origins.

"Our town was founded in the late 1800s by a remarkable woman named Lillian Farwell," Edward began, his voice rich with reverence. "A pioneer in the beekeeping industry, Lillian saw the potential in these rolling hills and the abundance of wildflowers that blanketed the landscape."

As he spoke, I hung on his every word, transported back in time by the vivid imagery he painted. Edward had a way of bringing history to life, infusing his tales with just the right balance of facts and anecdotes to keep his audience enthralled. And frankly, he wasn't bad to look at either. There was no way I was ready for a romantic relationship. But someday I would be.

Edward regaled us with stories of how the town had weathered tough times, from the Great Depression to World War II, each challenge only strengthening the resilient spirit of the community. By the time he finished, I felt a newfound appreciation for the town's roots and the pioneering spirit that had shaped its identity. His students must really enjoy hearing history from him. I bet he made it really fun for them.

Next up was Deb Richmond, a local storyteller known for her captivating tales of family legends and ghost stories. With a mischievous twinkle in her eye, she launched into a chilling account of the old Blackwood Mansion, perched atop one of the town's highest hills.

"They say the spirit of old Jeremiah Blackwood still roams the halls of that grand estate, searching endlessly for his lost love, Abigail," Deb intoned, her voice taking on a haunting quality. "Some claim to have seen ghostly lights flickering in the windows late at night, while others swear they've heard the mournful cries of a heartbroken man echoing through the grounds."

A collective shiver rippled through the room as Deb wove her haunting tale, each twist and turn drawing us deeper into the tragic love story. By the time she reached the climactic ending, in which Jeremiah's spirit was said to have faded away, finally reunited with his beloved Abigail in the afterlife, more than a few guests were dabbing at misty eyes.

As the evening progressed, the storytellers treated us to a delightful array of stories, each one offering a unique glimpse into the rich tapestry of Honeyridge Falls' history and lore.

Leonard Griffith, the gentleman with a passion for horology, regaled us with tales of rare timepieces he had collected over the years. One story, in particular, caught my attention--the legend of the Farwell Clock, an intricate antique timepiece rumored to contain a hidden compartment.

"The clock once belonged to Lillian Farwell herself," Leonard explained, his eyes shining with excitement. "Legend has it that she used the hidden compartment to stash away a key to a secret room."

Arthur took the floor next, sharing tales from his days as a private investigator that had the entire room hanging on his every word. He wove a gripping narrative about a case involving a stolen heirloom, a thrilling chase that had taken him through multiple towns.

"The key to solving any mystery," Arthur emphasized, "is to pay attention to the smallest details. Often, it's the seemingly insignificant pieces of evidence that hold the greatest revelations."

As he spoke, I found my mind whirring with possibilities and connections to Elena's case. Arthur's words only solidified my determination to leave no stone unturned in my quest for the truth.

Finally, it was Mrs. Whitaker's turn to share the legend of the Honeyridge Falls Locket, a story that had been passed down through generations. According to the tale, Lillian Farwell herself crafted the locket and imbued it with a powerful charm that would grant prosperity and protection to the town as long as her descendants possessed it.

"For years, the locket was passed down from mother to daughter, its magic safeguarding our little town from harm," Mrs. Whitaker intoned, her voice taking on a reverent hush. "But then, one fateful day, the locket disappeared, and with it, our good fortune seemed to fade."

My heart skipped a beat at the mention of the locket. I could have sworn that I had seen references to that somewhere before.

A heavy silence hung in the air as she finished her tale, each of us lost in contemplation of the mythical treasure and the implications of its disappearance. I couldn't help but wonder if the locket's vanishing had played a role in the recent tragedy that had befallen our community.

As the evening drew to a close and the guests dispersed, I lingered, my mind spinning with the weight of all the stories and legends I had heard. I felt as if a door had opened, revealing a glimpse into the rich tapestry of Honeyridge Falls' history, and allowing me to develop a deeper understanding of the community I had joined.

Lost in thought, I nearly jumped when a voice broke through my reverie.

"Moxie? Are you alright?"

I turned to find Edward Hawthorne standing beside me, his warm eyes filled with concern.

"Oh, yes, I'm fine," I assured him, offering a smile. "I was just lost in thought, processing all the incredible stories we heard tonight."

He nodded, a soft smile playing at the corners of his mouth. "It was truly a remarkable evening. Your grandmother has done an excellent job of reviving this tradition and reminding us all the importance of preserving our town's history."

"She has," I agreed, feeling a swell of pride for Grandma's efforts. "And I have to say, your storytelling skills are quite impressive, Mr. Hawthorne. You really brought the past to life for us. Your students must love you."

A faint blush crept into his cheeks at the compliment. "Please, call me Edward," he insisted. "And thank you, Moxie. I'm passionate about history. There's something deeply satisfying about uncovering the stories and legends that have shaped our community over the generations."

I nodded, understanding the sentiment all too well. "I feel the same way. Tonight has only deepened my appreciation for Honeyridge Falls and its resilient spirit."

We lapsed into a comfortable silence, both of us lost in our own thoughts for a moment. Then Edward cleared his throat, his expression taking on a hopeful cast.

"Moxie, I was wondering if perhaps you might like to join me for coffee sometime?" he ventured. "I'd love to discuss the town's history with you further, and maybe even get your input on some ideas I have for a local history project I'm working on."

I blinked, surprised by the invitation, but not altogether displeased. There was something about Edward's earnest enthusiasm and genuine love for the community that I found endearing.

"I'd like that," I heard myself saying before I could overthink it. "It sounds like it could be really interesting." Was I completely out of my mind? I wasn't that long out of a relationship with Chase.

Edward's face lit up with a warm smile that crinkled the corners of his eyes. "Wonderful! I'll look forward to it."

As he excused himself to mingle with the remaining guests, I felt a flutter of anticipation in my chest. Amidst the weight of the investigation and the lingering questions surrounding Elena's murder, Edward's invitation offered a welcome respite.

Gathering my thoughts, I made my way back to the great room where Grandma was tidying up the last of the refreshment trays.

Sneaker, ever the opportunist, perched on one of the tables and lapping up stray crumbs from the snacks.

"Sneaker!" I chided gently, scooping him up and nuzzling his soft fur. "You're going to make yourself sick if you keep indulging like that."

Grandma chuckled, shaking her head fondly at the mischievous feline. "That cat certainly has a sweet tooth," she remarked. "But I suppose we can't fault him for appreciating the finer things in life."

I smiled, cradling him against my chest as I surveyed the room, now empty save for the lingering traces of the evening's magic--the flickering fairy lights, the wildflower petals scattered across the tables, the faint aroma of honey and tea mingling in the air.

"Tonight was wonderful, Grandma," I said sincerely. "Thank you for reviving this tradition and giving me the chance to connect with the heart of Honeyridge Falls."

Her eyes shone with a mixture of pride and nostalgia. "It was my pleasure. Storytelling has always been a way for our community to come together, to share our histories and keep our traditions alive."

She paused, her gaze drifting to the empty chair beside the fireplace where Grandpa used to sit. "Your grandpa would have loved this event," she added softly, a gentle smile touching her lips. "He was quite the storyteller himself, you know. His vibrant personality and that hearty laugh of his would fill the room. He could turn even the simplest tale into an epic adventure. Oh, how he cherished these gatherings." Her eyes reflected the flickering lights, a tear gleaming momentarily before she brushed it away and continued to tidy up, her movements filled with a tender reverence for the past.

"I wish I could have heard more of his stories," I said, feeling a pang of longing mixed with affection.

As Grandma and I set about restoring the great room to its usual state, I replayed the evening's tales in my mind. The legend of the Farwell Locket, in particular, had piqued my curiosity, its mysterious disappearance and rumored powers lingering in the back of my mind like a puzzle waiting to be solved.

Chapter Twelve

As I pushed open the door, the Java Jive enveloped me in its bustle of activity. The gentle hum of conversation mingled with the soothing melodies of acoustic guitar music drifting through the speakers.

Making my way to the counter, a fresh-faced barista greeted me.

"Good morning!" he chirped, flashing me a warm smile that crinkled the corners of his eyes. "What can I get started for you today?"

I couldn't help but return his infectious grin, feeling a spark of appreciation for the newcomer's vibrant energy. "Good morning," I replied, scanning the chalkboard menu behind him. "I'll have a latte, but with an extra shot of espresso today, please."

The barista--Dominic, according to the embroidery on his crisp apron -- nodded in understanding. "Coming right up! This'll definitely kick-start your day," he assured me with a conspiratorial wink, already reaching for the well-worn porta filter.

As he set to work, I allowed my gaze to wander around the cozy space. A familiar figure caught my eye, tucked away in a corner booth with her laptop open before her. Decision time. Confront her about the botched press release or let it go?

The mix-up with the press release for the storytelling event still stung, and a part of me couldn't help but wonder if her error had been intentional, a subtle jab in our ongoing rivalry.

Before I could decide, Dominic's cheerful voice broke through my reverie.

"Here you go, one extra-strength coffee to start your day off right," he announced, sliding the steaming mug across the counter towards me. "Let me know if you need anything else!"

Murmuring my thanks, I cradled the warm ceramic in my hands, savoring the rich aroma that wafted up to greet me.

Decision made, I took a deep breath and made my way over to Sammy's secluded corner, my steps carrying me closer to the inevitable confrontation.

"Sammy," I began, my tone measured yet firm as I approached her table. "We need to talk."

The reporter's head snapped up at the sound of my voice, her eyes widening in surprise before narrowing ever so slightly, as if bracing herself for an impending clash. "Moxie," she acknowledged, her voice guarded. "What can I do for you?"

I slid into the booth across from her, setting my coffee mug down with a decisive clink against the worn tabletop. "I think you know exactly what this is about," I pressed, leveling my gaze at her. "The date mix-up for the storytelling event? Ring any bells?"

Her expression wavered, a flicker of remorse passing across her features before she schooled them into a mask of nonchalance. "Oh, that," she said with a dismissive wave of her hand. "It was just an honest mistake, Moxie. I had a million deadlines that week, and something must have slipped through the cracks."

Her cavalier attitude only stoked the embers of my frustration. "Really?" I challenged, arching an eyebrow. "Because it seems awfully convenient, given our history. Are you sure it wasn't just another one of your little digs at me?"

Sammy recoiled as if I'd struck her, hurt flashing across her face before being swiftly replaced by a flash of anger. "How dare you?" she hissed, her voice low and heated. "You think I would stoop that low, intentionally sabotaging an event just to get under your skin?"

Her vehement reaction gave me pause, and I searched her expression for any hint of deception. To my surprise, I found none--only raw emotion simmering beneath the surface.

Sensing my uncertainty, her shoulders slumped, and she heaved a weary sigh, raking a hand through her tousled locks. "Look, Moxie," she began, her tone softening. "I know we've had our differences, but you have to believe me when I say that the date mix-up was genuinely just a mistake."

She paused, worrying her lower lip between her teeth as if debating whether to divulge more. Finally, she met my gaze head-on, her eyes shimmering with a vulnerability I had never seen in her before.

"The truth is, my mom's been really sick lately," she confessed, her voice thick with emotion. "Cancer. It's been... really hard, juggling work and being there for her, you know? I've been distracted, and things have slipped through the cracks. That press release was just one of many balls I've dropped recently."

The weight of her admission hung heavy in the air between us, and I felt a wave of empathy wash over me, tempering the lingering embers of frustration. How could I have been so quick to assume the worst when Sammy was clearly struggling with a deeply personal battle?

"Sammy, I... I had no idea," I murmured, reaching across the table to give her hand a gentle squeeze. "I'm so sorry you're going through that. I shouldn't have jumped to conclusions."

She offered me a watery smile, her eyes glistening with unshed tears. "It's okay, I get it," she assured me, her voice wavering ever so slightly. "We haven't exactly been on the best of terms lately. But I want you to know that I would never intentionally get a story wrong. I strive for the utmost journalistic integrity."

In that moment, I saw Sammy not as a rival or a thorn in my side, but as a fellow human being navigating her own personal struggles with grace and resilience.

"Thank you for telling me," I said at last, giving her hand one final squeeze before releasing it. "And please, if there's anything I can do to help or support you during this time, don't hesitate to ask."

Her expression softened, and she nodded, offering me a grateful smile. "I appreciate that, Moxie, really. And you know, maybe there is something we could do to help each other out."

I arched an inquisitive eyebrow, intrigued by the shift in her demeanor. "I'm listening."

"Well, as you know, I have access to certain resources and information channels that the general public doesn't," she began, a familiar glint of determination sparking in her eyes. "What if I used those connections to dig a little deeper into Elena's case? See if I can uncover any leads or information that might have been overlooked?"

My heart skipped a beat at her suggestion, a flicker of hope igniting within me. With Sammy's journalistic skills and insider access, we might just stand a chance at uncovering the truth behind Elena's murder.

"That could be incredibly helpful," I admitted, leaning forward with renewed enthusiasm. "But won't the police have issues with us poking around in an active investigation?"

She waved a dismissive hand. "Leave the police to me," she assured me. "I have my ways of gathering information discreetly. The key is not to step on any toes or interfere with their work directly."

A conspiratorial grin tugged at the corners of her mouth. Even if her offer was self-serving to get a story, it would help me progress in solving Elena's case and make sure Chase wasn't arrested.

"Alright, Sammy," I agreed, holding her gaze. "Let's do this."

With that, we set about outlining a tentative plan of action. Sammy would leverage her network of contacts and sources to gather as much information as possible about Elena's past, her activities at the bee farm, and any potential leads.

In turn, I would continue my own discreet inquiries, sharing any insights or clues I uncovered with Sammy so that we could pool our resources and piece together a clearer picture of the events surrounding Elena's untimely demise.

As our impromptu strategy session drew to a close, I found myself filled with a renewed sense of purpose and determination.

"Thank you for this, Sammy," I said sincerely as we gathered our belongings to leave. "I know it can't be easy, juggling all of this on top of everything else you're dealing with."

She offered me a rueful smile, her eyes shining with a mixture of gratitude and weariness. "Don't mention it," she demurred. "Honestly, having something to focus on, a mystery to unravel, might just be the distraction I need right now."

As I made my way back to the B&B, my mind buzzed with renewed energy and purpose.

As I pushed open the door, the familiar scents of freshly brewed tea and baked goods enveloped me in a warm embrace. Grandma was bustling about the great room, tidying up the last remnants of the previous night's storytelling event.

"There you are, dear," she called out, her face lighting up with a warm smile as she spotted me. "I was wondering where you'd wandered off to."

I returned her smile, feeling a sense of contentment wash over me. "Just needed a little break to clear my head," I replied, crossing the room to give her a quick peck on the cheek. "But I'm feeling refreshed and ready to tackle whatever comes next."

Her eyes twinkled with a knowing look, as if she could sense the renewed determination coursing through me. "Well, that's just wonderful to hear," she said, patting my hand affectionately.

I couldn't help but chuckle. "I may have found an unexpected ally in my search for answers."

As I recounted my encounter with Sammy and our newfound partnership, she listened with rapt attention.

"Well, I'll be," she mused when I had finished. "Who would have thought that a little adversity could bring two stubborn souls like you and Sammy together?"

I shook my head in bemusement. "Certainly not me," I confessed. "But I have to admit, having her resources and connections on our side could be invaluable in cracking this case wide open."

Her eyes took on a faraway look. "You know, your grandpa used to say that the most unlikely alliances often prove to be the strongest," she mused.

"I think Grandpa was onto something," I said softly, feeling a renewed sense of appreciation. "And who knows? Maybe Sammy and I will end up surprising ourselves with how well we work together."

As Grandma headed toward the kitchen, I settled into a cozy armchair by the fireplace. My phone buzzed with a message from Sammy. I eagerly unlocked it to read her text.

"Hey Moxie," the message read, "I've already stumbled upon something promising. Need to verify it before I can give you the details, but feeling hopeful. Will keep you posted."

I hesitated. While her enthusiasm was infectious, a small voice of skepticism nagged at the back of my mind. Could she truly have found something substantial so quickly?

I typed out a measured response, careful not to dampen her spirits but also wary of getting too carried away.

"Thanks, Sammy. Looking forward to hearing more."

With a tap of my finger, the message was sent.

Chapter Thirteen

As the evening guests retreated to their quarters, I escaped to the small office tucked away behind the front desk.

I surveyed the makeshift investigation station I had assembled. Stacks of notes and printouts littered the desk. At the center of this organized chaos stood a large cork board, its surface a tangled web of colored yarn and pinned photographs, each string connecting the various suspects and potential motives in Elena's murder.

Sneaker hopped onto the desk, his green eyes regarding me with an almost quizzical expression as he surveyed the disarray before him.

"I know, I know," I murmured, reaching out to give his soft fur a gentle stroke. "It's a mess, but it's the only way I can make sense of it all."

With a contented purr, he settled onto a clear spot on the desk, his gaze fixed on me as if silently urging me to continue my musings aloud.

"Let's start with Chase," I began, plucking a photograph from the board and studying it intently. "My ex-boyfriend, the one person who should have had no reason to harm Elena, according to him. Yet, he's got to be a prime suspect." I shook my head, frustration creeping into my voice. "It just doesn't add up."

Sneaker tilted his head, his eyes seeming to bore into mine as if sensing the turmoil brewing within me.

"I mean, sure, he had a history of jealousy and possessiveness," I conceded, my finger tracing the yarn that connected Chase's photo to Elena's. "But murder? That's a whole different level of darkness that I can't quite reconcile with the man I knew."

A soft meow escaped Sneaker's throat, and I couldn't help but chuckle at his apparent commiseration.

"You're right, I'm getting ahead of myself," I acknowledged, setting Chase's photo aside for the moment. "Let's take a step back and look at the bigger picture."

My gaze swept over the array of faces pinned to the board, each one a puzzle piece in the tangled web of secrets and lies surrounding Elena's untimely demise. There was Adam, Elena's ex-boyfriend. And then there was Gabe, the disgruntled former employee whose termination from the bee farm had left him bitter and resentful. Had Elena played any role in that? Was that the secret Karen had mentioned?

As I studied their profiles, the picture felt incomplete.

A sudden knock at the office door startled me from my reverie, and I glanced up to find Jonathan hovering in the doorway.

I squealed and jumped at the interruption, my heart pounding a mile a minute.

"Apologies for the intrusion," he said, his voice a rich baritone. "Just saying hello."

I studied him, hoping he wasn't going to mention that someone had been in his room earlier. I had a great excuse with the towel delivery, but still. Maybe he had noticed his papers out of order.

I offered him a warm smile, gesturing for him to enter. "Not at all, Jonathan. Please, come in."

As he stepped into the office, his gaze swept over the chaotic array of evidence and notes, a flicker of recognition passing across his weath-ered features.

"Ah, I see you've adopted a rather unorthodox approach to your investigation," he observed, a hint of amusement coloring his tone.

I couldn't help but let out a self-deprecating chuckle. "Unorthodox is one way to put it," I agreed. "But when you're dealing with a tangled web of secrets and lies, sometimes a little chaos is necessary to make sense of it all."

He nodded sagely, his eyes lingering on the corkboard with its intricate tapestry of connections. "I can certainly appreciate the need for order amidst the chaos," he mused. "It's a process not unlike my own when crafting a new story."

My curiosity piqued, and I leaned forward, eager to glean any insights from the seasoned storyteller. "How so?"

A wistful smile tugged at the corners of his mouth as he settled into a nearby armchair. "Well, you see, my stories are rarely born from pure imagination," he began, his voice taking on a mesmerizing cadence. "More often than not, they find their roots in the fertile soil of real-life events, whispers of truth that I then weave into intricate tapestries of fiction."

I hung on his every word. "So, you take inspiration from actual occurrences?" Was he about to reveal more of what he knew about the bee farm? Could this help me connect some of my details together?

His eyes twinkled with a hint of mischief. "Inspiration, yes, but also far more than that," he elaborated. "You see, my dear, the true art lies in extracting the essence of a story from the raw materials of life -- the emotions, the motivations, the hidden truths that lurk beneath the surface of everyday existence."

I might just have to invite him to our next storytelling event. While he wasn't from Honeyridge Falls, his ability to entertain might be a great addition.

"It's almost as if you're conducting your own investigation," I murmured, my gaze flickering back to the corkboard and its tangled web of connections. "Piecing together fragments of reality to construct a cohesive narrative."

A slow, approving smile spread across his weathered features. "Precisely. And much like your own pursuit of the truth, my storytelling process often leads me down unexpected paths, uncovering layers of complexity that I hadn't expected."

He leaned forward, his eyes alight with a passion that seemed to transcend his years. "You see, Moxie, the art of storytelling is not merely about crafting entertaining tales--it's about holding a mirror up to the human condition, reflecting the depths of our emotions, our desires, our darkest impulses."

I found myself utterly transfixed.

"The characters we create, the narratives we spin--they are all reflections of the truths that lie within us, the hidden facets of our psyche that we often struggle to confront," he continued, his voice taking on a reverent quality. "And in exploring those truths through the lens of fiction, we sometimes stumble upon revelations that shake us to our very core."

A shiver of anticipation rippled through me as I considered the implications of his words. If Jonathan's stories were indeed rooted in reality, could they provide clues or insights into the very case I was grappling with?

"Have you ever stumbled upon truths that perhaps, were better left undisturbed?" I ventured, my voice tinged with a hint of trepidation.

His expression grew somber, his brow furrowing as he considered my question. "Alas, that is the double-edged sword we wield as seekers of truth," he acknowledged, his voice laced with a solemn gravity. "For every revelation that brings clarity, there is the risk of uncovering depths of darkness that might have been better left undisturbed."

A heavy silence settled between us, punctuated only by the soft purring of Sneaker, who had nestled himself contentedly at my side.

"But surely the pursuit of truth is worth the risk?" I pressed, my determination unwavering. "Isn't it better to shine a light on the shadows, no matter how unsettling the truth may be?"

He regarded me with a pensive gaze, his eyes betraying a lifetime of hard-won wisdom. "Perhaps," he conceded. "But one must also consider the ripple effects of such revelations, the unintended consequences that can reverberate through the lives of those touched by the truth."

His words hung heavy in the air, a sobering reminder of the delicate balance between uncovering the truth and preserving the fragile fabric of reality. I grappled with the weight of his caution, my resolve wavering ever so slightly.

As if sensing my inner turmoil, He leaned forward, his gaze piercing straight through to the depths of my soul. "Let me share a cautionary tale with you, my dear," he murmured, his voice taking on a hushed, conspiratorial tone.

I nodded, transfixed, bracing myself for the weight of the revelation he was about to impart.

"Years ago, when I was but a fledgling writer seeking to make my mark, I stumbled upon a story that captivated me--a tale of passion, betrayal, and ultimately, tragedy," he began, his eyes growing distant as he slipped into the currents of memory. "I became obsessed with uncovering every detail, every nuanced truth that lay beneath the surface of the sordid affair."

A tremor of foreboding rippled through me as he paused, his expression haunted by the ghosts of the past.

"The more I dug, the deeper I found myself entrenched in a web of secrets and lies that spanned decades," he continued, his voice barely above a whisper. "And in my relentless pursuit of the truth, I inadvertently set in motion a chain of events that would forever alter the lives of those involved."

My breath caught in my throat as the weight of his words settled upon me.

"What happened?" I breathed, scarcely daring to voice the question.

His eyes clouded with a profound sadness, a grief so palpable that it seemed to permeate the very air around us. "Families were torn asunder, lives were irreparably shattered," he murmured, his voice thick with remorse. "All because I could not resist the siren call of the truth, no matter the cost."

A deafening silence descended upon us, broken only by the faint ticking of the grandfather clock in the hallway.

"I've carried that burden with me ever since," he confessed, his gaze boring into mine with an intensity that sent a shiver down my spine. "And now, as I bear witness to your own relentless pursuit of the truth, I cannot help but fear that you, too, may confront consequences far graver than you ever imagined."

His words hung heavy in the air.

"I appreciate your words of caution," I said at last, my voice resolute. "But in this case, the truth is the only path forward. Too many lives have already been upended." I pointed toward my board. "Is there anything you see that stands out to you as critically important?"

"Physical evidence, Moxie," he began, his voice steady and contemplative. "It's the cornerstone of both criminal investigations and storytelling. It's not just about what's there, but often about what isn't there, or what seems too neatly arranged."

He paused, giving his words a moment to sink in. "Consider the murder weapon--the hive tool. It's a common enough item at a bee farm, yet it was found wiped clean of fingerprints. This suggests a calculated effort to remove traces, which is expected, but the placement of the tool itself? That's what caught my attention."

"What about the placement?" I asked, intrigued by the direction of his thoughts.

His gaze intensified. "If the attack was indeed a surprise, carried out from behind, one might expect some signs of a struggle, or at the very least, some disarray in Elena's immediate surroundings. Yet, the tool was conveniently placed next to her body, almost as if it was deliberately staged to be found. It doesn't quite add up."

He shifted slightly in his seat, the old chair creaking under his weight. "Consider the timing and location as well. The shed is secluded, used for storing beekeeping equipment, and the murder occurred late in the evening. This points to someone familiar with the farm's layout and schedule. But also to someone who knew how to navigate the area without attracting attention."

I nodded, my brain ticking over the new angles Jonathan had highlighted. "I'll take another look at the crime scene photos and check the reports again. Maybe there's something there that we all missed."

He smiled, a glint of satisfaction in his eyes. "Sometimes, it's not just about finding the truth; it's about questioning the stories that are too neatly told. Keep digging, and keep questioning."

"Thank you for your help," I said.

With a parting smile, he slipped from the office.

It was well past midnight when the shrill ring of the office phone pierced the stillness, shattering my reverie. With a start, I reached for the receiver, my heart pounding with a mixture of anticipation and trepidation.

"Sunny Honey Bed and Breakfast, this is Moxie speaking," I answered, my voice betraying none of the tumult churning within me.

"Moxie, it's Detective Wilson," came the familiar gruff voice on the other end of the line. "I apologize for the late hour, but I need to speak with you regarding the investigation into Elena's death."

My breath caught in my throat as a torrent of possibilities flooded my mind. Had they uncovered a crucial piece of evidence? Or perhaps apprehended a suspect? Why would they need to talk to me?

"Of course, Detective," I managed, willing my voice to remain steady. "What can I do for you?"

There was a pause, and I could almost envision the detective weighing his words carefully. "I'd prefer not to discuss the details over the phone," he said at last. "Could you come down to the station tomorrow morning? Say, around ten o'clock?"

A knot of apprehension twisted in my stomach, even as curiosity burned within me. "Certainly," I agreed, my fingers drumming an anxious rhythm on the desk. "I'll be there."

"Thank you," he replied, his tone betraying nothing.

The line went dead.

CHAPTER FOURTEEN

My hands trembled slightly as I gathered the stack of notes and photographs from my makeshift investigation board, meticulously arranging them into a leather-bound portfolio.

Steeling my resolve, I took a deep breath and turned towards the doorway, where Grandma stood watching me with a mixture of concern and unwavering support etched across her weathered features.

"You don't have to do this alone," she murmured, her voice a soothing balm. "I'll be right by your side, every step of the way."

A grateful smile tugged at the corners of my lips as I regarded the woman who had become an anchor amidst the turbulent currents of this unfolding mystery. "Thank you," I replied, my voice thick with emotion. "I don't know what I'd do without you."

With a reassuring pat on my arm, she ushered me towards the front door.

The drive to the police station passed in a blur, my mind a whirlwind of thoughts and possibilities. What could Detective Wilson possibly want from me? Had they uncovered some damning piece of evidence that implicated me in Elena's murder? Or was this simply a routine follow-up, a standard procedure in their ongoing investigation since my name and number had been found in Elena's purse?

Before I could spiral further into the depths of speculation, the imposing façade of the police station loomed before us. Taking a steadying breath, I followed Grandma through the heavy oak doors and into the bustling heart of the precinct.

The atmosphere was electric, a palpable tension hanging in the air as uniformed officers scurried about. My steps faltered momentarily, but Grandma's reassuring presence propelled me forward, her hand resting gently on the small of my back as we approached the front desk.

"Moxie Rayburn, here to see Detective Wilson," I announced, my voice wavering ever so slightly.

The desk sergeant regarded me with a cool, appraising gaze before consulting his computer terminal. "He's expecting you," he confirmed with a curt nod. "Down the hall, third door on the left. You can wait there."

With a murmured thanks, I followed his directions, the echo of our footsteps reverberating like a mournful drumbeat against the stark walls. As we reached the door, Grandma's hand found mine, giving it a gentle, reassuring squeeze.

"Wait here," she instructed, her tone brooking no argument. "I'll have a word with the detective before we proceed."

Before I could protest, she had slipped through the door, leaving me alone in the corridor with only the distant hum of activity to keep me company.

"I wonder what they want?" I mumbled.

The muffled sound of raised voices from beyond the door shattered the fragile calm of the hallway. I strained to make out the words being exchanged. Grandma's familiar tones, laced with a steely determination, clashed against the gruff baritone of Detective Wilson, their heated exchange punctuated by the occasional thud of a fist striking a desk.

Just as I contemplated the wisdom of intervening, the door swung open, and Grandma emerged, her expression a mask of grim triumph. "Come along, dear," she beckoned, her voice leaving no room for argument. "The detective is ready to see us now."

With a fortifying breath, I rose to my feet and followed her into the interrogation room. The space was spartan, its bare walls and harsh fluorescent lighting lending an almost clinical ambiance to the proceedings.

Detective Wilson sat behind a battered metal desk, his features carved into a stern visage as he regarded us with an appraising gaze. "Ms. Rayburn," he greeted, his tone clipped and professional. "Thank you for coming in."

I opened my mouth to respond, but Grandma beat me to the punch, her voice ringing with a maternal ferocity that brooked no opposition. "Of course she came," she retorted, her eyes blazing with a protective fire. "But I'll be staying right here, by her side, for the duration of this... interview."

A muscle twitched in the detective's jaw, but he offered a terse nod of acquiescence. "Very well," he conceded, gesturing towards the chairs arranged before his desk. "Please, have a seat."

As we settled into the rigid metal chairs, Grandma's hand found mine once more, her grip reassuring and unwavering. Detective Wilson regarded us for a long, weighted moment before leaning forward, his gaze boring into mine with an intensity that sent a shiver rippling down my spine.

"Ms. Rayburn, I'm going to be direct with you," he began, his voice low and grave. "In the course of our investigation into Elena Martinez's murder, certain... discrepancies have come to light that implicate you as a potential suspect."

The words hung in the air like a physical weight, pressing down upon me with suffocating force. A thousand protestations of innocence clamored for release, but before I could give voice to any of them, Grandma had already sprung to my defense.

"Discrepancies?" she scoffed, her tone laced with derision. "I hardly think my granddaughter's efforts to uncover the truth and bring justice for a senseless murder constitute grounds for suspicion, Detective."

Detective Wilson's jaw clenched, but he pressed on, undeterred. "Your involvement in this case goes beyond mere amateur sleuthing, Ms. Rayburn," he countered, his gaze flickering towards the portfolio clutched in my white-knuckled grip. "You've been conducting your own investigation, gathering evidence, and inserting yourself into matters that are better left to the professionals."

A flicker of indignation flared within me, lending strength to my voice as I finally found the courage to speak up. "With all due respect, Detective, I'm not just some meddlesome busybody," I retorted, my words laced with conviction. "I have a personal stake in this case. Elena was involved with my ex-boyfriend, Chase Donovan."

The detective's brow furrowed, and he leaned back in his chair, regarding me with a mixture of skepticism and begrudging interest. "Go on," he prompted, his tone guarded.

Emboldened by his apparent willingness to listen, I launched into a detailed account of my findings thus far, laying out the tangled web of connections and potential motives that I had uncovered. As I spoke, I could sense the weight of Grandma's pride, her unwavering faith in me a tangible force that buoyed my spirits and lent conviction to my words.

Yet, as my narrative reached its conclusion, Detective Wilson's expression remained inscrutable, his features carved into an impassive mask that betrayed nothing of his thoughts or intentions.

"An intriguing theory, to be sure," he conceded at last, his voice measured and even. "But I'm afraid it does little to assuage our concerns about your potential involvement in this matter."

A ripple of unease coursed through me, and I leaned forward, my grip on the portfolio tightening reflexively. "What do you mean?" I pressed, my voice tinged with a hint of trepidation.

The detective's gaze was unwavering, his eyes boring into mine with an intensity that sent a shiver down my spine. "Let's start with your connection to the victim," he began, his tone taking on a clinical detachment. "Elena Martinez was intimately involved with your ex-boyfriend, Chase Donovan--a fact that you've readily admitted. Now, while you claim to harbor no ill will towards either of them, we cannot discount the possibility of lingering resentment or jealousy playing a role in your actions."

Grandma bristled beside me, her posture radiating indignation, but I laid a calming hand on her arm, silently imploring her to let me handle this. "Detective, I won't deny that the situation with Chase and Elena was... complicated," I acknowledged, choosing my words with care. "But any feelings of hurt or anger I might have harbored were in the past. I'd moved on, and my sole motivation in pursuing this case was to uncover the truth and ensure justice was served."

The detective regarded me for a long moment, his expression inscrutable, before continuing. "Be that as it may, we cannot ignore the fact that your alibi for the time of the killing is... shaky, at best."

A cold tendril of dread snaked its way down my spine as the weight of his words settled upon me.

"That's preposterous!" Grandma erupted, her voice ringing with righteous indignation. "Moxie was with me the entire evening. Her alibi is iron-clad!"

But Detective Wilson remained unmoved, his expression carved from granite as he leveled his gaze at me once more. "I'm afraid the timelines don't quite add up, Ms. Rayburn," he stated, his words carrying the weight of grim certainty. "According to multiple witness statements, there were periods throughout the evening where your whereabouts were unaccounted for, windows of opportunity, if you will."

The air seemed to grow thinner, each breath a struggle as the implications of his words washed over me like a suffocating wave.

Sensing my distress, Grandma wrapped a protective arm around my shoulders, her voice taking on a soothing maternal cadence as she sought to bolster my wavering resolve. "Now, now, let's not get ahead of ourselves," she murmured, her gaze never wavering from the detective's impassive countenance. "Surely there's a reasonable explanation for these supposed gaps in Moxie's alibi. She's been nothing but forthcoming and cooperative throughout this entire ordeal."

But Detective Wilson remained unmoved, as he regarded us both with a scrutiny that bordered on accusation. "I'm afraid reasonable explanations hold little weight in the face of hard evidence, ma'am," he countered, his voice laced with a grim finality. "And the evidence we've uncovered thus far paints a rather damning picture."

A heavy silence descended upon the room, punctuated only by the thunderous pounding of my heart against my ribcage. I could feel the weight of suspicion pressing down upon me, suffocating and inescapable, threatening to crush the very breath from my lungs.

Drawing upon every ounce of resolve I could muster, I straightened my spine and met the detective's gaze head-on, my voice ringing with a conviction that belied the turmoil roiling within me.

"Detective, I understand the gravity of the situation, and I appreciate the need for thoroughness in your investigation," I began, my words measured. "But I can assure you, with every fiber of my being, that I had no part in Elena's death." I knew my word wasn't enough. But right now it was the best I could do.

I pressed on. "I won't deny that there may be gaps or inconsistencies in my alibi. But to accuse me of murder?" I shook my head, my voice ringing with conviction. "That's a bridge too far, Detective."

For a fleeting moment, I thought I detected a flicker of respect in the detective's steely gaze, a begrudging acknowledgment of the unwavering resolve that burned within me. But it was gone in an instant, replaced by the impassive mask of professionalism that had become his hallmark.

His tone brought no argument. "I'm instructing you to remain available for further questioning and to refrain from any activities that could be construed as obstructing our efforts."

The weight of his words settled upon me like a physical burden, but I refused to be cowed. With a resolute nod, I met his gaze unflinchingly. "You have my full cooperation, Detective," I assured him, my voice steady and unwavering.

A tense silence hung in the air. Finally, he inclined his head in a curt acknowledgment, his expression inscrutable.

"That will be all for now, Ms. Rayburn," he dismissed, rising from his chair and effectively signaling the end of our interview. "You're free to go, but I expect your full cooperation should we require your presence again."

As we made our way out of the interrogation room and back into the bustling heart of the precinct, I couldn't help but feel a sense of relief mingled with a renewed determination.

Grandma's hand found mine once more, her grip steadfast and reassuring as we stepped out into the crisp autumn air. "You handled yourself admirably in there, my dear," she murmured, her eyes shining with a mixture of pride and maternal concern.

I nodded. "Thank you." Was the detective just pressuring me to see if I would give something up about Chase? Did they suspect he really did it?

CHAPTER FIFTEEN

The hum of the engine and the blur of passing scenery seemed to mirror the whirl of my thoughts. "It's hard, isn't it?" Grandma said, breaking the silence that had settled between us like a heavy fog. "Facing all those accusations, feeling like you're under a microscope."

I sighed, nodding as I watched the trees lining the road sway gently in the breeze. "It's like no matter what I say, it's never enough. They just keep digging and digging, looking for something that isn't there."

"They have to follow every lead, Moxie. It's just how these things go," she said.

Her words, warm, and confident, helped ease the tightness in my chest. "Thanks," I murmured. "I'm trying. It's just hard to keep the faith sometimes."

As we turned into the driveway of the B&B, a thought struck me, a welcome distraction from the relentless tension of the day. "I think I need to do something... productive. Get my mind off all this for a bit."

"Oh?" her voice was tinged with curiosity as she glanced at me. "What do you have in mind?"

"There's something Mrs. Whitaker mentioned at the storytelling event about Lillian Farwell, one of our town founders. She had this locket that supposedly held some kind of secret. I'm thinking of hitting the library to see if there's anything I can dig up on it."

A smile spread across her face, her eyes lighting up. "That sounds like a fantastic idea."

I felt a flicker of excitement at the prospect, my spirits lifting slightly. "Yeah, I think so too."

I dropped Grandma off and returned to town. As the Honeyridge Falls Library loomed before me, I felt the weight upon my shoulders ease ever so slightly.

Stepping through the ornate double doors, the familiar scent of aged paper and the hushed stillness that seemed to permeate every nook and cranny of the cavernous space greeted me.

A soft clearing of a throat drew my attention towards the circulation desk, where a bespectacled figure regarded me with a warm, welcoming smile. "Welcome," the man greeted, his voice a rich, melodic timbre. "I'm CJ. How may I assist you today?"

Mustering what composure I could, I offered a tentative smile in return. "Good afternoon, CJ," I began, my voice tinged with a hint of trepidation. "I was hoping to delve into some of the town's historical records, particularly anything pertaining to a locket that may have been connected to the town's founding."

His eyes sparkled with undisguised interest, his brow furrowing ever so slightly as he processed my request. "A locket, you say?" he mused, tone laced with a mixture of curiosity and intrigue. "That's certainly an intriguing line of inquiry. I'd be delighted to assist you in your research."

Relief washed over me at his willingness to aid my quest, and I offered him a grateful nod. "Thank you," I murmured, my voice brimming with a newfound sense of purpose. "I would appreciate any guidance you can provide."

With a warm smile, CJ beckoned me to follow him, leading me through a labyrinth of towering shelves and hushed alcoves until we reached a secluded corner of the library.

"These are our historical archives," he explained, his voice taking on a reverent hush as he gestured towards the floor-to-ceiling shelves that lined the walls. "Every record, every document, every scrap of information pertaining to the town's history can be found within these hallowed stacks."

A thrill of anticipation rippled through me. Without a second thought, I rolled up my sleeves and plunged into my search. I scoured the shelves for any clue about the mysterious locket and its ties to the town's founding.

Hours seemed to blur together as CJ and I pored over dusty volumes and faded manuscripts. Just when I thought we had reached a dead end, a faded photograph caught my eye, its sepia tones lending an air of timeless elegance to the image it captured.

"CJ, look at this," I breathed, carefully extracting the fragile photograph from its protective sleeve. "Isn't that?.."

The librarian leaned in, his eyes widening in recognition as he studied the image. "Why, yes," he murmured, his voice tinged with awe. "That's Lillian Farwell, the town's founder, wearing what appears to be an ornate locket around her neck."

A surge of excitement rippled through me as the pieces fell into place. "This must be the very locket Mrs. Whitaker was referring to," I exclaimed, my voice hushed yet brimming with triumph. "But what could its significance be? And why would it be so closely tied to the town's founding?"

As if in answer to my query, CJ carefully extracted a tattered sketch-book from one of the shelves, its pages yellowed and brittle with age. "I also found this," he murmured, carefully turning the delicate pages until he reached a faded pencil sketch that seemed to depict a crude map.

I leaned closer, my eyes roving over the intricate details etched upon the aged parchment. A winding creek seemed to converge upon a solitary 'X' marked amidst a copse of trees, and I felt a frisson of excitement dance along my spine as the implications of this discovery sank in.

"Could this be showing the location of the locket?" I breathed, my finger tracing the path of the meandering waterway.

CJ regarded the sketch with a thoughtful expression. "It's certainly a possibility," he mused. "Seems worth checking out."

I pulled out my phone and snapped a few pictures of our finds. This might be just the distraction I needed. And how fun to explore the town's history, and possibly even get answers to some long-standing questions.

"Well?" he prompted, his voice laced with an undercurrent of adventure.

"I've got to check this out," I said, holding up my phone.

"I'd love to help, if you're open for a sleuthing partner," he said. "Put my research skills to use in a real life quest."

I laughed, grateful for the break in the seriousness of the investigation. "Sounds good. Thank you so much for your help."

We retraced our steps from the archives to the front door. This excursion did wonders to lift my mood. And I was so happy to make a new friend in town. I thanked CJ for the help and exited the staleness for some fresher air.

As I rounded the corner onto Main Street, a sight awaited me that caused my heart to plummet into the depths of my stomach. It was the unmistakable figure of Chase, his hands bound behind his back as a pair of grim-faced officers led inside him.

The world seemed to tilt on its axis, my breath catching in my throat. Shock, disbelief, and a lingering tendril of hurt all vied for dominance.

I could only stand there, rooted to the spot. Had the police uncovered damning evidence against Chase? Was my visit with Detective Wilson in any way part of this arrest? Did I say the wrong thing to get him arrested?

As Chase's figure disappeared behind the imposing doors of the precinct, I squared my shoulders, my jaw set in a resolute line. "I don't know what's going on," I murmured, my voice trembling ever so slightly with the weight of conviction. "But I intend to find out."

I had to regroup. This was not good.

Hurrying back to the B&B, I rushed in. "Grandma," I hollered as I entered.

"Moxie?" she murmured, rising from her chair and making her way towards me. "What's wrong?"

"It's Chase," I managed, my voice trembling with a potent mixture of disbelief and lingering hurt. "I saw him being led into the police station in handcuffs. They must have found evidence implicating him in Elena's murder."

"Oh, my dear girl," she murmured.

I leaned against the soft fabric of her blouse, my eyes squeezed shut as I willed the burning sting of tears to subside. "I don't know what to think," I confessed, my voice muffled by the embrace we shared. "A part of me wants to believe in his innocence. But another part can't help but wonder if there was a side to him."

"One step at a time," she said, patting my back.

Slowly, I extricated myself from her embrace. "I have to go see him."

"Are you sure that's a good idea?" she asked.

"I have to see in person to find out for sure if he really did this." I straightened my shoulders with much more bravado than I felt.

"Let me go with you," she offered, grabbing her coat.

"No. I need to do this alone." I paused. "Chase knows you're not his biggest fan."

"I'm not, and for good reason. But I still wouldn't want an innocent man to pay for something he didn't do. Even Chase," she said.

"I need to do this alone," I repeated firmly as I headed towards the police station. The evening air was crisp. My mind raced with countless scenarios.

I hesitated at the entrance, taking a deep breath before pushing the door open.

"I'm here to see Chase Donovan," I said, trying to sound more confident than I felt.

The officer on duty looked up, his expression unreadable. "Are you family?"

"No, but I'm--"

He raised a hand, cutting me off. "Only family members are allowed visitation after hours, ma'am."

Desperation clawed at me. "Please, it's important. I just need a few minutes." I clasped my hands together, pleading.

He studied me for a long moment, then sighed and nodded. "Alright, five minutes. But that's it."

I followed him through a series of secured doors until we reached the visitation room. It was stark and cold, with a glass partition separating visitors from inmates. Chase was already there, his face drawn and tired. He looked up as I entered, and for a moment, his stoic facade faltered.

"Moxie," he breathed, his voice muffled by the glass. We picked up the phones simultaneously.

"Chase, what's going on?" I asked, the worry clear in my voice.

He shook his head, a mixture of frustration and fear in his eyes. "I didn't do it, Moxie. I swear to you, I didn't kill Elena."

The certainty in his voice shook me. "But they must have evidence--"

"It's not what it looks like. Believe me," he pleaded, his hand pressing against the glass. "I know it sounds crazy, but I didn't do this."

His words hung in the air, heavy and implausible. My heart raced, but doubts lingered, fueled by unanswered questions. "Chase, why didn't you tell me you worked at the bee farm with Elena? That's important, and you hid it from me."

His eyes widened slightly, the color draining from his face. "I... I thought it would look bad. I didn't want you to think--"

"That what? That you were involved?" My voice rose, tinged with hurt and suspicion.

"I was afraid it would complicate things more than they already were. I didn't kill her, Moxie, but I knew how it looked. We were just colleagues, nothing more."

"Why should I believe you?" The question came out harsher than I intended, driven by a tumult of emotions.

"Because you know me, Moxie. You know who I am, and you know I couldn't do something like this," he said, his voice steady despite the desperation in his eyes.

His expression turned somber, the weight of the situation sinking in. "Chase, do you have any idea who might have wanted Elena dead?" I pressed, needing to grasp at any lead that could unravel the truth.

He hesitated, his eyes darting away before locking back on mine with a troubled look. "The only person I can think of is Adam," he confessed, his voice barely above a whisper. "Elena's ex-boyfriend. He was devastated when he found out about us."

"Devastated enough to kill?" I asked, the question hanging heavily in the air.

He shifted uncomfortably, the clank of his handcuffs echoing in the small room. "I don't know. He was furious. As soon as he found out she was having an affair with me, he dumped her. He felt betrayed by both of us."

The pieces of a complex puzzle were forming, but with each piece, the image grew darker, more convoluted. "Did he confront you?"

"Yeah, he did. More than once. He said things... things that scared Elena." Chase looked down, his hands clenched. "She told me he threatened her, said he'd make her pay for ruining everything."

The officer at the door signaled that time was up. Chase's eyes held mine, imploring me to trust him. "Please, Moxie, find out the truth. I didn't do this, but maybe Adam..."

Chapter Sixteen

The heavy metal door clanged shut behind me, its finality echoting through the cold, sterile hallway. Chase's anguished expression seared into my mind.

The crisp air hit my face as I stepped outside, pulling my jacket tighter against the chill. Doubt swirled within me like a gathering storm.

I squeezed my eyes shut, willing the cacophony of thoughts to quiet. Deep down, I knew Chase. The man I had fallen for all those years ago--passionate, principled, with an unwavering moral compass that had drawn me to him like a moth to a flame.

Flashes of our time together flickered through my mind's eye--lazy Sunday mornings spent lounging, the way his eyes would crinkle at the corners when he laughed. How could I reconcile those cherished memories with the grim reality that now confronted me?

Pulling out my phone, I hesitated. Was I relying too much on my connection with Sammy? Could this somehow backfire? No, I dismissed the thought. Her sharp reporter instincts and extensive contacts were exactly what I needed right now.

She answered on the first ring, her voice brisk and concerned. "Meet at Bumble Brews?" she suggested immediately. I agreed and set off, deciding to walk the several blocks to the bar to clear my head. We needed space to think, plan, and figure out how to get Chase out of this mess.

By the time I pushed through the door, the familiar jingle of the bell and the cozy aroma of the place wrapped around me, offering a slight ease to my tension. I ordered two beers at the counter--Sammy's and mine--before choosing a table in a quiet corner.

I had just set down the drinks when Sammy burst through the door, her eyes scanning the room until they landed on me. Her expression was a mix of concern and determination as she made her way over.

"Moxie!" she called out, her tone tinged with urgency as she slid into the seat across from me. "I came as soon as I could. What's going on?."

My eyes welled up as Sammy settled in across from me, her presence making the reality of the situation hit even harder. I took a deep breath, trying to steady my voice.

"It's... it's really bad, Sammy," I managed, blinking back tears. "Chase is in deep trouble, and he swears he didn't do it. I--I just don't know what to do." My voice cracked under the strain, and I reached for my beer, hoping the cool liquid might calm the storm inside me.

Sammy's brow furrowed, her lips pursing in contemplation. "But you don't sound convinced," she observed astutely, her gaze holding mine with an intensity that bordered on unnerving.

I sniffled and sipped my beer. "I just don't know anymore."

She leaned forward, her expression shifting to one of sharp focus as she saw my distress. Pulling out a small notepad and a pen from her bag, she clicked the pen, ready to jot down notes.

"Okay, Moxie, let's break this down," she began, her tone businesslike, cutting through the emotional fog. "First, what exactly are the charges against Chase? And what evidence do the police have?"

She paused, giving me a moment to compose myself before continuing. "We need to know everything that's being said and done. Chase's side of the story, the timeline of events leading up to the arrest, any witnesses, everything. The more details we have, the better we can understand the situation and figure out our next move."

Sammy's transition into her reporter mode was swift and precise, grounding me back into the reality that we had a job to do--clear Chase's name.

"He told me that Adam, who works at the bee farm, was Elena's boyfriend," I said.

Sammy looked up, her eyes sparking with the thrill of a lead. "That's great info, Moxie," she said, already thinking several steps ahead. "If Adam was involved with Elena, he could have a motive. We need to find out where he was around the time of Elena's death, talk to people at the bee farm, see if anyone noticed anything unusual about his behavior."

Her determination was contagious, and it bolstered my spirits just enough to believe we might find something that could help Chase.

I nodded, leaning closer as the weight of Chase's predicament pressed upon me. "Chase said Adam was devastated when he found out about the affair. He confronted both of them, made threats against Elena." My voice dropped to a hushed whisper, the gravity of the situation lending a somber undertone to my words. "We need to look into Adam, see if he had the means and opportunity to commit the crime."

"Who would know Adam's movements and state of mind during that time?" Sammy asked, her brow furrowing in thought. "We should start by questioning his closest friends, coworkers, anyone he might have confided in or spent time with."

I considered her words, mentally running through the potential sources in our small town. "Frankly, I think we should start with co-workers. After all, Elena was found at the farm."

Sammy nodded, making a note. "Good idea."

"When I was there for the setup the other day, I met several of the farm workers." I sat up straighter. "We should attempt to talk to as many as we can. I would guess the police have already done that. But maybe with friendly faces, they might open up more."

"Sounds like a plan," Sammy agreed, a determined glint in her eye. "We'll have to be subtle, though."

My mind raced, plotting out potential strategies for gathering information discreetly. "At the festival, we could split up and mingle with the different groups," I suggested. "You could chat up the vendors, maybe pose as a food blogger interested in their honey-based products. I could strike up conversations with the workers, play the part of a newcomer returning to town after many years."

Sammy's eyes lit up at the idea. "Ooh, I like it! I can be the bubbly, overly enthusiastic foodie, peppering them with questions about their recipes and processes. Maybe I'll even bring along a fake camera crew for extra credibility."

I couldn't help but chuckle at the mental image, a spark of hope flickering to life within me. "And I'll be the wide-eyed newbie, soaking in all the local lore and traditions," I added, already envisioning the perfect cover story.

Sammy's fingers drummed an eager staccato against the tabletop. "Leave it to me," she declared, her voice brimming with confidence. "I'll dig into Adam's background, see what I can unearth about his movements and potential motives."

Relief washed over me, a tentative spark of hope igniting within my chest. But a nagging voice in the back of my mind whispered cautions, reminding me not to let my desires cloud my judgment.

"But we need to be discreet," I said, my gaze darting around the bustling café as if fearing prying eyes and ears. "If Adam is involved, we don't want to tip him off and risk him fleeing or destroying evidence."

Her expression sobered, her head bobbing in solemn agreement. "Of course," she murmured, her voice dropping to a conspiratorial whisper. "We'll have to be careful. Play our cards close to the vest."

As the details of our plan solidified, a weight lifted from my shoulders.

With our plan taking shape, I glanced at my phone, realizing how quickly time had passed. "I should get back," I said. "I've got a night shift to cover."

Without letting my hopes get too high, I returned home.

The hours ticked by, stretching before me like an endless expanse. I busied myself with menial tasks to pass the time.

The shrill trill of my phone pierced the stillness, and I fumbled to answer, grateful for the distraction. "Hello?"

"Moxie, it's Arthur." The rich, familiar timbre washed over me.

"Arthur," I greeted, my voice betraying a hint of trepidation. "What's going on? Have you uncovered something new about the case?"

There was a pause, a weighted silence that seemed to stretch interminably before he spoke again. "I've been looking into Chase's alibi," he began, his tone measured and devoid of emotion. "And I have to say, the picture isn't looking good for him."

My heart sank, a leaden weight settling in the pit of my stomach. "What do you mean?" I pressed, my fingers tightening around the phone until my knuckles turned white.

Arthur's sigh crackled through the line. "His alibi for the night of the murder is shaky at best," he explained, his voice tinged with a hint of regret. "And the more I dig into his relationship with Elena, the more it seems like he had a powerful motive to keep their affair under wraps."

The words hit me like a physical blow, stealing the breath from my lungs. Could it be true? Had Chase been lying to me all along? A flood of memories came back--sneaking off together, whispering sweet nothings, and a deep belief that we knew each other's true selves.

Had it all been a lie?

"I know you want to believe in him, Moxie," Arthur continued, his voice softening ever so slightly. "But the evidence is mounting, and you need to prepare yourself for the possibility that he might not be the man you thought he was."

As the call ended, I found myself adrift in a sea of doubt and uncertainty. A place I didn't want to go.

A soft meow at my feet drew my attention downward. Without a word, I scooped Sneaker up, burying my face in his soft fur as a solitary tear traced a glistening path down my cheek. He seemed to sense just when I needed him most.

He purred contentedly.

As the night wore on, Arthur's words echoed in my mind.

The plan Sammy and I had concocted for the Honey Festival took on a newfound significance. It just had to work. My last chance to find the actual killer, or to confirm the unthinkable truth about Chase's guilt.

Chapter Seventeen

The Honeyridge Falls Honey Festival was in full swing. Sammy and I arrived early to take in the opening ceremonies and get our bearings to divide and conquer the investigation. A festive energy crackled through the crisp morning air, mingling with the tantalizing aroma of honey-glazed treats and the gentle hum of bees.

Mayor Wilkins, resplendent in a canary yellow pantsuit, took the stage with a broad grin. "Welcome, one and all, to the 75th annual Honey Festival!" she boomed, her voice ringing out over the cheering crowd. "A beloved tradition that celebrates the sweet heart of our community and the hard-working bees that make it all possible."

I shifted from foot to foot, my mind only partially focused on the mayor's words. Sammy, ever the consummate professional, scribbled notes in her trusty reporter's pad, her eyes alight with determination.

"And of course, we mustn't forget the highlight of our festival," Mayor Wilkins continued, pausing for dramatic effect. "The crowning of our Queen Bee in just one hour's time!"

As the opening ceremonies drew to a close, Sammy leaned in close. "Okay, you hit up Karen at the bee farm booth. See if you can get her to open up about Adam's behavior leading up to the murder," she murmured, her voice low and conspiratorial. "I'll mingle with the other workers, see what I can dig up."

I nodded, a renewed sense of purpose straightening my spine. "Be careful," I cautioned, my brow furrowing with concern. "If Adam is involved, we don't want to spook him."

Sammy's eyes danced with a mixture of excitement and trepidation. "Don't worry about me," she assured me, her voice brimming with confidence. "I've got this."

With a final nod, we parted ways, weaving through the crowds of festival-goers. I made my way towards the bee farm booth, my heart pounding with a mix of nerves and anticipation. Karen welcomed me with a beaming smile.

"Moxie!" she greeted, her eyes twinkling. "Welcome back. What can I get for you? Didn't everything turn out great?" She gestured broadly at the bustling scene around us. The festival setup was indeed impressive, and the air buzzed with the energy of happy attendees.

I matched her smile, though I was here for more than just pleasantries. "Actually, Karen, I was hoping to pick your brain about something."

"OK," she replied, stepping closer. "What's on your mind?"

I kept my tone light, though my inquiry was anything but casual. "It's about Adam. I heard he's been having a tough time lately." I hoped my straightforwardness wouldn't deter her from sharing.

Her expression turned serious, and she glanced around before leaning in. "Poor Adam," she whispered, a note of genuine concern in her voice. "He's been a mess since he found out about Elena. Those two were together for ages until he discovered she ..."

My interest peaked at the mention of Elena's name. "Really?" I responded, pretending to be shocked.

She nodded gravely. "Absolutely. Adam was devastated. I mean, they had their whole life planned out." She paused, her eyes clouding over with thought. "And since then, he's been so changed. Distant, moody. It's like he's lost his spark."

A chill ran down my spine as I processed her words. Could Adam's erratic behavior be a sign of guilt? Or was he simply overwhelmed by the loss of his girlfriend? A pang of sympathy tugged at my heart.

Before I could press further, a familiar voice cut through the din of the festival. "Well, well, if it isn't our resident amateur sleuth."

I whirled around to find Detective Wilson sauntering towards us, a smug grin plastered across his face. His crisp uniform seemed out of place amidst the casual festivity, a stark reminder of the gravity of the situation.

"Detective," I greeted him coolly, my jaw clenching involuntarily.

"Come to enjoy the festival, have we?" he drawled, his eyes glinting with amusement. "Or are you still chasing ghosts, trying to prove your boyfriend's innocence?"

My cheeks flushed with a mixture of anger and embarrassment. Boyfriend? The word felt like a slap. I swallowed hard, forcing down the lump that had formed in my throat.

"He's not my boyfriend," I retorted, struggling to keep my voice level.

Brandon let out a derisive chuckle. "The truth is that we have Chase dead to rights," he proclaimed, his confidence unwavering. "The evidence against him is overwhelming. You'd do well to accept that and move on."

His words stung, reigniting the embers of doubt that had been smoldering within me. What if Arthur was right? What if Chase had been lying to me all along, and I was too blinded by my feelings to see the truth?

Gritting my teeth, I mustered what little composure I had left. "With all due respect, Detective, I'll be the judge of that," I countered, my tone clipped and resolute.

He merely shrugged, his expression one of infuriating smugness. "Suit yourself," he conceded. "But don't say I didn't warn you."

With a final, dismissive glance, he turned on his heel and strode away, leaving me seething in his wake. Karen laid a gentle hand on my arm, her eyes filled with sympathy.

"Don't mind him," she soothed.

I managed a tight smile, grateful for her kindness.

"Thank you," I murmured, my voice thick with emotion.

As I made my way through the bustling festival grounds, my mind whirled with conflicting thoughts and emotions. Sammy waved me over from a secluded corner, her expression grave.

"What did you find out?" I asked, my heart pounding with a mixture of trepidation and hope.

Sammy's brow furrowed as she recounted her findings. "According to the other workers, Adam's been acting erratically ever since Elena's death," she began, her voice low and urgent. "He's been prone to outbursts, showing up late or not at all. A few of them even mentioned hearing him arguing with someone on the phone, though they couldn't make out the details."

My breath caught in my throat as the pieces fell into place. "Karen said something similar," I confided, my voice hushed. "Apparently, Adam and Elena were planning a future together. Until they weren't."

Sammy nodded, her face serious. "There's more. First, Derek, a local vendor who knew Elena well. He mentioned Elena had been unusually secretive recently. She was seen having hushed conversations with unknown visitors, looking anxious whenever someone questioned her plans."

"Did Derek have any idea what she might have been hiding?" I asked.

"Not exactly," Sammy replied, shaking her head. "But he felt whatever it was, it could put her at odds with someone close. He thinks she was involved in something big, something she wanted to keep under wraps."

"Anyone else?" I asked.

"Right, Keith," she continued. "He's been observing Adam's recent behavior, and it's not looking good. Keith caught him in a heated phone call that sounded pretty intense. According to Keith, Adam has been struggling a lot since Elena's death."

Sammy's eyes widened, and she opened her mouth to speak, but a commotion nearby caught our attention. A couple of workers had gathered near the storage shed, their voices raised in heated argument.

"That's Adam," Sammy breathed, her gaze fixed on the confrontation unfolding before us.

Without a word, we crept closer, careful to remain out of sight. Adam stood toe-to-toe with a petite woman, her face contorted with rage.

"You need to let her go, Adam," the woman hissed, her voice trembling with barely contained emotion. "Elena's not coming back."

Adam's shoulders slumped, his expression a mask of weary resignation. "Tessa, please," he pleaded, his tone tinged with exasperation. "We've been over this a thousand times. It's never going to work between us."

My heart stuttered in my chest as the pieces fell into place. Tessa Caldwell.

Tessa's eyes flashed with a dangerous intensity. "You don't mean that," she insisted, her voice rising in pitch. "I know you have feelings for me, Adam. You're just too scared to admit it."

Adam recoiled as if struck, his face contorting in a mixture of pity and revulsion. "Tessa, you're deluding yourself," he countered, his words laced with a weary finality. "I've never had feelings for you."

With each heated exchange, Tessa seemed to unravel further, her composure slipping away like water through cupped hands. I leaned forward, every fiber of my being straining to make sense of the bizarre confrontation playing out before me.

Tessa's lips twisted into a snarl, and she took a step closer, her hands balling into tight fists at her sides. "You'll regret this, Adam," she spat, her voice dripping with venom. "Mark my words, you'll be sorry you ever crossed me."

A shudder rippled through me at the naked threat in her words. This woman was unhinged, consumed by a twisted obsession that had clearly spiraled out of control. Beside me, Sammy stiffened, her sharp reporter's instincts no doubt picking up on the same chilling undercurrent.

"Do you think...?" Sammy began, her voice hushed and uncertain.

I nodded slowly, the pieces finally falling into place with a sickening finality. "Tessa was obsessed with Adam," I murmured, my heart hammering in my chest.

Adam took a deep breath, stepping closer to Tessa with a gentleness that surprised me. "Tessa, listen to me," he began, his voice soft but firm. "You've been a good friend, and I don't want to lose that. But you have to understand, what we had was never..."

Tessa's eyes softened, and she blinked rapidly, as if trying to hold back tears. "I know, Adam, but you've been so distant since Elena died. I just want to be there for you, to help you through this."

Adam reached out and placed a comforting hand on her shoulder. "I appreciate that, Tessa. I really do. But my feelings for you... they're not what you think."

Tessa looked down, her shoulders shaking. "You're just confused, Adam," she insisted, her voice trembling with hope. "You've been through so much. It's okay to need someone. It's okay to need me."

Adam's expression hardened slightly, and he took her hands in his, holding them firmly. "Tessa, I care about you. But not in the way you want. I need you to understand that."

Tessa's face fell, her hopeful expression darkening into one of anger and frustration. She yanked her hands from Adam's grip, her eyes blazing with a mixture of hurt and fury. "No," she snapped, her voice rising. "You don't get to do this to me, Adam. Not after everything."

Adam took a step back, his own face showing a flicker of concern. "Tessa, please. I'm not trying to hurt you. I just need you to understand."

Tessa's lips twisted into a bitter smile. "Understand what? That you'll never see me as anything more than a friend? That I'm not good enough for you?"

"No, that's not it at all," Adam protested, his voice pained. "You're a wonderful person, Tessa. But I can't force myself to feel something that isn't there."

She laughed, a harsh, mirthless sound. "So, you're just going to keep pushing me away, pretending like you don't need anyone?"

Adam's jaw tightened. "It's not about needing someone. It's about being honest with ourselves."

Tessa's eyes narrowed, and she took a threatening step forward. "You think you can just brush me off like I don't matter? Like I haven't been there for you through everything?"

Adam held his ground, his voice steady but firm. "I'm not brushing you off. I'm being honest. We both deserve to be happy, Tessa. But this isn't the way."

Tessa's hands balled into fists at her sides, her whole body trembling with rage. "You'll regret this, Adam. Just wait and see. You'll come crawling back to me when you realize you need me."

Adam sighed, a look of sadness crossing his face. "I don't want things to end like this between us. But you have to let me go."

Her eyes flashed dangerously, and she spat out her next words with venom. "You'll regret it. I swear, you'll regret it."

Chapter Eighteen

As Tessa's words grew more heated, her veiled threats sending chills down my spine, the loudspeaker crackled to life, momentarily cutting through the tension. "Attention, festival-goers!" Mayor Wilkins' booming voice rang out. "The crowning of our Queen Bee is about to begin! Please make your way to the main stage!"

A collective murmur of anticipation swept through the crowd, and the masses began to shift and flow towards the central gathering point. Sammy and I exchanged a loaded glance, our eyes wide with the weight of what we'd just overheard.

"We need to do something," Sammy whispered urgently, her gaze darting between Adam, Tessa, and the oblivious throngs of people milling about.

I nodded, my mind racing to formulate a plan. "You go find Detective Wilson," I instructed, my voice low but firm. "I'll stay here and try to keep Tessa engaged until you get back."

Sammy's brow furrowed with concern, but she gave a curt nod before melting into the crowd, her reporter's instincts guiding her steps. Taking a deep breath, I turned my attention back to the confrontation unfolding before me.

Tessa's face contorted into a mask of fury, her eyes blazing with a dangerous intensity. "You'll regret this, Adam," she spat, her words dripping with venom. "Mark my words, you'll be sorry you ever crossed me."

Adam's expression was one of weary resignation, tinged with a hint of pity. "Tessa, please," he implored, his voice strained but gentle. "I never meant to hurt you, but this obsession has gone too far."

Tessa recoiled as if struck, her nostrils flaring with indignation. "Obsession?" she echoed, her voice rising in pitch. "Is that what you think this is? I love you, Adam. Can't you see that?"

Adam shook his head slowly, his gaze sorrowful. "What you're feeling isn't love, Tessa. It's an unhealthy fixation, and it's tearing you apart."

Tessa's lips twisted into a bitter sneer. "So, what, you think you can just dismiss my feelings like they don't matter?" She took a step closer, her body trembling with barely contained rage. "After everything we've been through together?"

Adam held his ground, his expression a mixture of sadness and resolve. "Tessa, I care about you, but not in the way you want."

Tessa's eyes narrowed to slits, and she let out a harsh bark of laughter. "So, that's it, then? You're just going to toss me aside like I'm nothing? Like that cheating Elena meant more to you than me?"

A flicker of anger passed over Adam's features at the mention of Elena's name. "Don't bring her into this," he warned, his voice taking on a sharper edge.

But she was relentless, her words lashing out like whips. "What, you still carrying a torch for your precious Elena?" she sneered. "Even after she betrayed you? Even after she got what she deserved?"

My heart stuttered in my chest as the implication of her words sank in. Tessa knew more about Elena's death than she was letting on.

Sensing an opening, I stepped forward, my hands raised in a placating gesture. "Tessa," I began, my tone measured but firm. "What are you saying? Do you know something about what happened to Elena?"

She whirled on me, her eyes wild and unfocused. "Stay out of this," she warned, her words slurred with emotion. "This is between me and Adam."

I held her gaze, my heart pounding in my chest. "I can't do that, Tessa," I replied, my voice steady despite the tremor of fear that coursed through me. "Not when an innocent man is sitting in jail for a crime he didn't commit."

Her expression morphed from rage to confusion, and for a fleeting moment, I saw a glimmer of vulnerability in her eyes. But just as quickly, it was gone, replaced by a steely resolve that sent a chill down my spine.

"Innocent?" she scoffed, her lips curling into a contemptuous sneer. "You mean Chase? Please, that lying snake is as guilty as they come."

My breath caught in my throat as the pieces fell into place. Tessa's twisted obsession had targeted Chase, the man I had once loved and the one whose innocence I had been fighting so desperately to prove.

"You don't know anything," Tessa spat, her words laced with a dangerous edge.

Adam took a tentative step forward, his hands raised in a placating gesture. "Tessa, please," he implored, his voice thick with emotion. "Don't do anything you'll regret. Chase had nothing to do with this."

Tessa's gaze snapped back to him, her eyes blazing with a mixture of hurt and fury. "Regret?" she echoed, her voice trembling with barely contained rage. "You want to talk about regret?"

She let out a harsh, mirthless laugh, her shoulders shaking with the force of her emotions. "The only thing I regret is ever thinking you could love me back," she seethed, her words cutting like knives. "After everything I did for you, after I got rid of that lying, cheating Elena so we could finally be together..."

The words hung in the air, heavy and damning, as the full weight of her confession sank in. Adam's face drained of color, his eyes wide with shock and disbelief.

"You..." he breathed, his voice little more than a hoarse whisper. "You killed Elena? And framed Chase for it?"

Tessa's expression wavered, a flicker of uncertainty crossing her features before her mask of bravado slipped back into place. "She deserved it," she spat, her voice laced with a twisted sense of righteousness. "She was going to ruin everything we had. And Chase..." She let out a derisive snort. "He was just collateral damage, a convenient scapegoat to take the fall."

A wave of nausea washed over me as the full scope of Tessa's depravity came into focus. Not only had she killed Elena in a fit of delusional jealousy, but she had also framed an innocent man, allowing Chase to languish in jail while the true culprit walked free.

Before I could react, a commotion behind me caught my attention. Sammy emerged from the crowd, Detective Wilson in tow, his expression one of grim determination.

"Tessa Caldwell," he called out, his voice ringing with authority. "You're under arrest for the murder of Elena Martinez and the false imprisonment of Chase Donovan."

Tessa's eyes widened, and for a moment, she looked like a cornered animal, her gaze darting wildly from side to side. Then, without warning, she bolted, her feet pounding against the grass as she fled towards the treeline.

"Stop her!" Wilson barked, breaking into a sprint in pursuit.

Without thinking, I took off after them, my heart hammering in my chest as adrenaline coursed through my veins. Tessa may have had a head start, but I was fueled by a burning sense of justice--not just for Elena, but for Chase as well.

Weaving through the maze of tents and vendors, I caught glimpses of Tessa's retreating form, her hair streaming behind her like a banner in the wind. Ahead, Wilson was gaining ground, his face set in a mask of grim determination.

As we neared the edge of the festival grounds, Tessa made a desperate lunge towards a cluster of trees, her eyes wild with desperation. But

Wilson was faster, his years of training and experience giving him the edge he needed.

With a well-timed tackle, he brought Tessa crashing to the ground, the impact knocking the wind from her lungs. She thrashed and fought. But Wilson's grip was like iron, his handcuffs snapping into place with a finality that sent a wave of relief washing over me.

Sammy skidded to a halt beside me, her chest heaving with exertion. "We got her," she panted, her eyes wide with a mixture of triumph and disbelief. "We finally got the truth."

I nodded, my breath coming in ragged gasps as the adrenaline subsided. "It's over," I murmured, the weight of those two simple words settling over me like a heavy mantle. "Chase is finally going to be free."

As Wilson hauled Tessa to her feet, her eyes met mine, and in that moment, I saw a flicker of something else beneath the rage and obsession--a haunting emptiness, a void where her humanity should have been.

"Why, Tessa?" I asked, my voice laced with a mixture of pity and revulsion. "Why go to such extremes? Why frame an innocent man?"

Tessa's lips twisted into a bitter sneer, her eyes glinting with a dangerous madness. "Because he was in my way," she spat, her words dripping with possessive venom. "Elena was going to take Adam away from me, and Chase was just..." she trailed off, a contemptuous shrug rolling her shoulders.

A shudder rippled through me at the twisted logic behind her actions. This was no crime of passion, but a calculated act of violence born from a twisted, obsessive love that had festered and metastasized into something truly monstrous.

Wilson called another deputy to lead Tessa away. She held her head high in a final act of defiance. I felt a strange sense of hollowness settle over me. Justice had been served, the truth laid bare, but at what cost? How many lives had been irrevocably shattered in the wake of Tessa's madness?

Sammy laid a gentle hand on my arm, her eyes filled with a mixture of sadness and understanding. "You did it, Moxie," she murmured, her voice thick with emotion. "You solved the case and cleared Chase's name."

I managed a tight smile, my thoughts drifting to Chase. "Chase never deserved any of this."

Sammy nodded, her expression somber. "Some things can't be undone," she acknowledged, her words ringing with hard-won wisdom. "But at least now, the truth is out there."

As we made our way back to the festival grounds, the sounds of laughter and celebration a jarring contrast to the gravity of what had just transpired, I couldn't help but feel a sense of relief mingled with a lingering sadness and guilt.

"Detective, what should we do now?" Mayor Wilkins asked, her voice tense with worry. "Should we continue with the festival?"

Wilson, scanning the crowd for any further disruptions, nodded firmly. "Yes, Mayor, proceed with the coronation. We've handled the situation here."

Relief washed over Mayor Wilkins's face as she straightened her sash. "Very well. We'll carry on with the Queen Bee coronation then. Thank you."

We made our way to the main stage, where the atmosphere was markedly different from the tension-filled scenes of just a bit ago.

Banners of gold and black, with artfully painted buzzing bees, festooned the stage. Mayor Wilkins stepped up to the microphone, her voice booming as she called the festival back to order.

"Ladies and gentlemen, thank you for your patience and understanding," she began, her tone both commanding and comforting. "Let's continue to celebrate the spirit of our community and the hard work of our beekeepers. It is my pleasure to proceed with the crowning of this year's Queen Bee, Miss Emily Carter!"

Applause erupted from the crowd as Emily, a bright-eyed teenager in a sparkling bee-themed gown, stepped forward. The crowd transformed the earlier tension into a moment of pure celebration.

Emily waved to the audience, her smile radiant under the stage lights. Sammy nudged me, slipping back into her role as a reporter with seamless professionalism. "I need to get some comments from the crowd and the new Queen Bee."

Chapter Nineteen

A soft hum of conversation filled the air, punctuated by the occasional clink of glasses and the melodic laughter of the guests gathered for our impromptu celebration.

I couldn't believe that only a few hours had passed since the chaos of the Honey Festival.

I leaned against the plush cushions of the loveseat, letting the weight of the day's events finally settle over me.

Betty and George were engaged in an animated discussion with Cora Harper, the local antique dealer.

Across the room, Grandma and Arthur sat side by side, their fingers intertwined in a subtle display of affection that spoke volumes. A tender smile played across Grandma's lips.

A warm weight settled against my leg, and I glanced down to find Sneaker nestled beside me, his eyes half-lidded in a picture of feline bliss.

"Quite the day, wasn't it?"

I looked up to find Sammy, an unlikely ally, sliding onto the loveseat beside me.

"That's an understatement," I replied.

"And I got a great story out of it," she said, her reporter mode never far away. "Adam told me he discovered Elena had been steeling honey. That she was working with someone to develop some kind of youthful cream with it."

"So that was her big secret?" I asked.

"Yeah. I guess she'd been doing it for quite a while. The owners were also about to fire her," Sammy added.

"Wow. There was so much going on there," I said. "I almost imagined the actual killer might never be caught. That Chase..."

Sammy followed my line of sight, her expression softening. "You did good, Moxie." she murmured.

A pang of conflicting emotions stirred within me at the mention of Chase's name. Relief but also a lingering sadness for the injustice he had endured, all because of Tessa's twisted obsession.

As if summoned by my thoughts, Chase appeared in the doorway.

Excusing myself from Sammy's company, I rose to my feet and made my way towards him, my heart thrumming with a complicated cadence of emotions. Relief and gratitude, tempered by the knowledge that too much had transpired for us to ever truly go back.

"Chase," I breathed, coming to a halt before him.

His lips curved into a tentative smile, his eyes searching mine for a glimmer of hope. "Moxie," he murmured, his voice thick with emotion. "I can't begin to thank you for everything you've done. You risked so much to prove my innocence, and I'll be forever grateful."

I nodded, my throat constricting with a swell of conflicting emotions. "You never deserved any of this, Chase," I managed, my voice trembling slightly. "What Tessa did to you, to Elena... it was unforgivable."

Chase's expression darkened momentarily, a flicker of pain crossing his features at the mention of Elena's name. "I know," he murmured, his gaze holding mine with an intensity that sent a shiver down my spine. "But you... you never gave up on me, even when it seemed like the whole world did."

He reached out, his fingers brushing against my cheek in a tender caress that stirred a riot of conflicting emotions within me. "After everything that's happened, it might seem impossible. But Moxie, I still love you. And if you'll have me, I'd like nothing more than to start over, to build something new together."

His words hung in the air, heavy with promise and possibility. A part of me yearned to say yes. To cast aside the pain and heartbreak of the past and embrace the chance at a fresh start.

Steeling my resolve, I met Chase's gaze with a mixture of tenderness and firm resolution. "Chase, you'll always hold a special place in my heart," I began, my voice thick with emotion. "But too much has happened for us to simply pick up where we left off."

His expression faltered, a flicker of disappointment clouding his features. But to his credit, he held my gaze.

"During this entire ordeal, I've learned so much about myself," I continued, my words flowing with a newfound sense of clarity. "I've discovered a strength and resilience that I never knew I possessed. And as much as a part of me will always love you, I know now that my path lies elsewhere."

He nodded slowly, his lips curving into a bittersweet smile. "I understand," he murmured, his voice laced with a quiet acceptance. "And as much as it pains me, I respect your decision."

A weight seemed to lift from my shoulders. Impulsively, I stepped forward and wrapped my arms around him, pulling him into a fierce embrace.

"Thank you," I whispered, my words laden with a depth of emotion that transcended the boundaries of our past. "Thank you for understanding."

As we parted, Chase offered me a final, tender smile before turning and slipping back through the doorway.

A soft weight pressed against my leg. Somehow, that cat knew just what I needed.

"Well, my furry friend," I murmured, my voice thick with a mixture of emotions. "It seems we've both embarked on a new chapter, haven't we?"

Straightening my shoulders, I turned and made my way back towards the gathering, my steps lighter than they had been in weeks.

As my gaze swept over the familiar faces of the B&B's residents and staff, I was struck by a profound sense of belonging. These people, this place, had become more than just a temporary haven--they had become my community, my chosen family.

A gentle hand on my arm drew me from my reverie, and I turned to find Grandma regarding me with a tender smile. "You look pensive, my dear," she murmured.

"Just reflecting on how far I've come," I admitted, my voice laced with a quiet awe. "I see you and Arthur are getting closer," I said softly, an affectionate tease laced through my words.

Her cheeks took on a gentle pink hue, her smile widening. "Oh, Moxie," she chuckled, her eyes twinkling with something I recognized as a mixture of joy and bashfulness. "Arthur has been a wonderful friend, especially through all the tumult."

I would leave it for now. But those two had something going on.

As the evening wore on, guests bid their farewells.

I found myself in the cozy confines of the B&B's library, a crackling fire casting flickering shadows across the walls. Sneaker was curled at my feet, his soft snores a soothing accompaniment.

A soft knock at the door drew my attention, and I glanced up to find Detective Wilson framing the doorway, his expression one of quiet satisfaction.

"Mind if I join you for a moment?" he asked, his voice carrying a hint of weariness that spoke to the long hours he had undoubtedly put in over the course of the investigation.

I gestured towards the plush armchair opposite me, offering him a warm smile. "Of course, Detective. Please, make yourself comfortable."

He settled into the chair with a grateful sigh, his gaze drifting towards the crackling flames. For a few moments, a comfortable silence stretched between us, punctuated only by the occasional crackle of the fire and Sneaker's soft snores.

"I have to admit, Moxie," he began at last, his voice low and contemplative. "You played a key role in solving the case."

"At least justice was served in the end," I murmured, drawing strength from the certainty of those words. "Chase is finally free, and Tessa will face the consequences of her actions."

His smile widened, a hint of amusement sparkling in his eyes. "Life has a way of taking unexpected turns, doesn't it?" he mused, leaning back in his chair.

He chuckled, "Just don't make it a habit to get involved in police investigations."

I held up both hands. "Nope. This is all your bailiwick."

He stood and shook my hand. Quite the formality. With a contented sigh, I settled deeper into the plush cushions of the armchair, a respite from the excitement of the case.

A soft knock at the front door drew me from my reverie, the sound echoing through the hushed stillness. Frowning slightly, I glanced at the antique clock adorning the mantle, its hands indicating a late hour. Was this a new guest I had forgotten was arriving?

Curiosity piqued, I rose to my feet, Sneaker stirring at my movement and blinking up at me with a sleepy gaze. "Stay here," I murmured, scratching behind his ears. "I'll go see who our late-night caller is."

As I reached for the doorknob, a sense of foreboding flickered through me. Taking a steadying breath, I pulled open the door, my eyes widening in surprise at the sight that greeted me.

A woman stood on the doorstep, her features partially obscured by the shadows cast by the porch light. Her posture was ramrod straight, exuding an air of quiet determination that sent a shiver of anticipation down my spine.

"Miss Rayburn?" she inquired, her voice carrying a faint lilt. "I'm terribly sorry to disturb you at this hour, but I couldn't resist the opportunity to meet you in person."

I blinked, taken aback by her formal demeanor and the intensity of her gaze. "I'm afraid you have me at a disadvantage," I replied, recovering my composure with a polite smile. "And please, call me Moxie."

The woman inclined her head in a subtle gesture of acknowledgment. "Moxie, then," she murmured, her lips curving into an enigmatic smile. "My name is Elise Farwell, and I've come a long way to seek your assistance."

A frisson of curiosity rippled through me at her words, my mind already spinning with possibilities. "My assistance?" I echoed, my brow furrowing slightly in puzzlement.

Her smile deepened, taking on an almost conspiratorial quality. "At your recent storytelling event, there was talk of a locket belonging to one of my relatives," she explained, her voice dropping to a hushed murmur. "This heirloom has been passed down through generations. And I had hoped to finally find it."

My breath caught in my throat as the pieces fell into place.

"You know something about the locket?" I pressed, my voice tinged with a mixture of curiosity and disbelief.

Her expression grew somber. "If the stories are true, it may hold the answers to a mystery that has plagued my lineage for generations."

Steeling my resolve, I met her gaze with a determined gleam in my eye. "Then we had better start at the beginning," I said, my voice ringing with a quiet confidence.

As I ushered Elise inside, the weight of her words lingered in the air. A new chapter was unfolding. Would I be solving two mysteries in one day?

Chapter Twenty

I inhaled deeply as the aroma of freshly brewed coffee and the sizzle of bacon on the griddle filled the air. I couldn't believe that only a few short weeks had passed since I had arrived here, my heart heavy with the weight of heartbreak and uncertainty.

Now, as I sipped my steaming mug of coffee, the events of the previous night replayed in my mind like a vivid dream. Elise Farwell's unexpected arrival carried the promise of a new mystery to unravel.

"You're up early this morning, dear."

Grandma's voice, laced with a hint of gentle concern.

"I couldn't sleep," I admitted, setting my mug down on the worn wooden table. "A woman named Elise Farwell showed up late last night, claiming to be a descendant of Lillian Farwell."

Grandma's brow furrowed, her expression one of puzzlement. "Lillian Farwell?"

I nodded, leaning forward in my chair. "She's the original owner of that locket we learned about during Mrs. Whitaker's story," I explained, my words tumbling forth in a rush of excitement. "The one that's been passed down through generations, but remains missing."

Understanding dawned in Grandma's eyes, her lips parting in a silent 'oh' of realization. "And this Elise claims to be a descendant of Lillian's?" she asked.

I nodded, the weight of Elise's words still fresh in my mind. "She believes that the locket holds the answers to some long-standing mystery within her family's history," I continued. "And she's come here in the hopes of finding it."

A silence settled over us, punctuated only by the distant clatter of dishes and the muted hum of conversation from the dining room. Finally, Grandma spoke.

"Well," she said. "It seems we have a new mystery on our hands."

"You're right," I affirmed, my voice ringing with a newfound sense of purpose. "And fortunately, I may already have a lead on where to begin our search."

Her eyebrows arched inquisitively, silently prompting me to continue.

I explained, leaning forward in my chair. "I visited CJ at the library, hoping he might have some insight or historical records that could shed light on the mystery."

Her expression brightened, her eyes alight with a mixture of pride and intrigue. "That boy always had a knack for uncovering the most obscure bits of local lore," she mused, a fond smile playing across her lips.

I nodded, my excitement building. "Well, it turns out CJ came across an old sketch in one of the library's archives," I continued. "It looks like a map or set of clues leading to its location."

Her eyes widened. "Goodness, Moxie," she breathed. "It seems you've stumbled upon a veritable scavenger hunt!"

I couldn't help but grin at the infectious enthusiasm that radiated from her.

"CJ and I agreed to meet later today, after his shift at the library," I continued, my words tumbling forth in a rush of anticipation. "We're going to study the sketch more closely and see if we can figure out where the locket might be."

Grandma sat back in her chair, the lines of her face softening into a thoughtful expression.

"Moxie," she began, her tone shifting to one of caution, "have you considered the possibility that this Elise might not be who she claims to be?"

I paused, the sudden question catching me off guard. "What do you mean?"

She set her cup down with a gentle clink. "It's just that it's rather convenient, don't you think? A woman shows up out of the blue, claiming to be a descendant of Lillian Farwell, right after Mrs. Whitaker talked about it at the storytelling event."

I frowned, considering her words. "You think she might be an imposter?"

She nodded slowly, her eyes narrowing slightly as she leaned forward. "There are people who would go to great lengths to get their hands on something as potentially valuable as that locket."

"But she seemed so genuine," I protested, although doubt crept into my voice.

"Why don't you and CJ look into the archives a bit more?" she said. "See if there's any record of Lillian having descendants or any other family who might corroborate this Elise's story?"

"That's a good idea," I said, feeling a renewed sense of purpose. "We'll start there."

"You know," Grandma started. "With the success of the storytelling event, I think we should plan something else."

I blinked, momentarily taken aback by the sudden shift in conversation. "What did you have in mind?"

A sly grin spread across grandma's face as she leaned back in her chair. "Oh, I'm not sure yet," she mused, tapping her chin thoughtfully. "But I think we should brainstorm a few ideas."

I couldn't help but chuckle at her infectious enthusiasm. "Alright," I agreed, settling back in my chair. "Let's hear your ideas."

For the next few minutes, a flurry of suggestions filled the air, each one more outlandish and delightful than the last. She proposed a community bake-off, with prizes awarded for the most creative and delicious confections. Then, she pivoted to the idea of a historical reenactment, complete with period costumes and elaborate set pieces.

I found myself caught up in the whirlwind of possibilities, my mind racing to keep pace with her boundless creativity. We entertained notions of a classic car show, a talent showcase, and even a quirky pet parade--an idea that had us both dissolving into fits of laughter at the mental image of Sneaker strutting his stuff alongside a menagerie of furry companions.

Finally, she said, "You know, I think we might be overthinking this."

I arched an eyebrow. "What do you mean?"

Her lips curved into a knowing smile. "Moxie, my dear, we already have the perfect event idea staring us right in the face," she declared, her words carrying the weight of realization. "A scavenger hunt."

I blinked, momentarily taken aback by the simplicity of her suggestion.

"You're a genius," I said, my mind already whirring with possibilities.

She waved a dismissive hand, her cheeks flushed. "Oh, pish-posh, my dear," she chuckled, her eyes twinkling with mirth.

A sudden commotion from the hallway shattered the tranquil atmosphere, the sound of a piercing scream echoing through the B&B. We exchanged a startled glance.

We hurried towards the source of the commotion, our footsteps echoing against the hardwood floors. As we rounded the corner, a scene of chaos and confusion greeted us.

Guests had spilled out into the hallway. At the center of the gathering stood Marjorie, one of our housekeepers, her face ashen and her eyes wide with shock.

"What in heaven's name is going on?" Grandma demanded, her voice cutting through the din of murmured speculation like a clarion call.

Marjorie turned towards us, her hand trembling as she pointed towards an open doorway further down the hall. "It's Mr. Norris," she stammered, her words tumbling forth in a breathless rush. "He's... he's..."

A chill ran down my spine as the implication of her words sank in. Without a moment's hesitation, I stepped forward, my heart pounding in my ears as I approached the open doorway.

What greeted me was a scene straight out of a macabre nightmare.

Sprawled on the floor, his body contorted in an unnatural pose, lay the still form of a man. A crimson stain seeped across the plush carpet, trailing outward from a gash on the side of his head that seemed to gape accusingly.

A collective gasp rippled through the gathered crowd.

"Moxie, dear God..." Grandma's voice, laced with a mixture of horror and sorrow, broke through the cacophony.

I turned to face her, my expression one of grim determination. "Call Detective Wilson," I instructed, my voice steady despite the turmoil of emotions roiling within me. "I'm not sure this was an accident."

As the words left my lips, a chorus of hushed whispers erupted from the gathered guests, their voices laden with a mixture of fear and morbid curiosity.

"Didn't he just check in last night?"

"I thought I heard an argument coming from his room..."

"But he was alone, wasn't he?"

As the murmurs of shocked guests filled the air, I stepped forward. "Please, everyone, head downstairs," I said, trying to steady my voice. "We'll have breakfast soon. Let's give the authorities space to work."

The guests moved reluctantly. They shuffled toward the stairs, and I waited until the last of them had cleared the area before turning back to the grim scene in the room.

We stepped just inside the threshold of the deceased man's room, careful not to disturb anything.

My eyes scanned the room, noting every detail--the disheveled sheets on the bed, the half-open suitcase near the wardrobe, and a solitary photograph that had fallen to the floor by the nightstand. I bent down to pick it up, my fingers trembling as I turned it over.

It was an old black-and-white photo, showing a young woman with a radiant smile and a man who looked strikingly similar to our deceased guest. On the back, faded ink read: "To Iris, all my love forever, Silas."

A jolt of surprise ran through me. I turned to Grandma, who was peering over my shoulder at the photograph. For a moment, her face was unreadable, but then her mouth twitched and her eyes narrowed--a quick flash of emotion crossed her features.

"Grandma?" I asked, my voice low but firm. "Do you know this man?"

She inhaled deeply, her fingers brushing against the photo as if pulled by some unseen force. "Silas and I... we knew each other long ago," she finally admitted, her voice a whisper. "It was another lifetime."

NEXT RELEASE

A quiet morning erupts when a dead body is found at the Sunny Honey B&B. The victim's connection to her grandmother, Iris, sends shockwaves through Honeyridge Falls. Reluctantly teaming up with the local detective, Moxie dives into a whirlwind investigation to clear her grandmother's name and save the B&B.

As Moxie unravels a web of secrets, lies, and red herrings, she discovers the victim's complicated past, including a previous marriage and estranged relationships. Tense confrontations, cryptic notes, and a mysterious letter hint at a deeper conspiracy. Just when Moxie thinks she's close to solving the case, an unexpected twist changes everything, revealing hidden connections and shocking motives.

"Murder at the B&B" is a cozy mystery filled with heart, humor, and suspense. Join Moxie Rayburn on her thrilling quest for justice in Honeyridge Falls, where every clue leads to new twists and turns that will keep you guessing until the very end.

About the Author

Hello from the cozy corners of my imagination! I'm Sue Hollowell. If we were meeting in person, you'd probably find me offering you a slice of cake (extra frosting, because life's too short!) and reminiscing about the playful antics of my beloved spaniels.

Having an empty nest filled me with an abundance of memories and affection, looking for an outlet. With time on my hands and a head full of stories, I ventured into the enchanting realm of writing.

Stay tuned, and get ready to dive into worlds filled with mystery, charm, and more than a few surprises.

www.ingramcontent.com/pod-product-compliance
Lightning Source LLC
Chambersburg PA
CBHW021955120726
47992CB00001B/264